A Christmas Quilt

"Merry Old Santa Claus" by Thomas Nast, 1881

A Christmas Quilt

A Quilters Club Mystery
(The Prequel)

Marjory Sorrell Rockwell

ABSOLUTELY AMA⚡ING eBOOKS

ABSOLUTELY AMAZING eBOOKS

Published by Whiz Bang LLC, 926 Truman Avenue, Key West, Florida 33040, USA.

For information contact:
Publisher@AbsolutelyAmazingEbooks.com

ISBN-13: 978-1945772207 (Absolutely Amazing Ebooks)
ISBN-10: 1945772204

A salute to all the real Leslie Anns
who are learning to quilt ...

Other Quilters Club Mysteries
By Marjory Sorrell Rockwell

The Quilters Club Quartet

The Underhanded Stitch

The Patchwork Puzzler

Coming Unraveled

Hemmed In

Sewed Up Tight

All Tangled Up

Available from
AbsolutelyAmazingEbooks.com

A Christmas
Quilt

Part 1

First of the Three Spirits

"The curtains of his bed were drawn aside, I tell you, by a hand. Not the curtains at his feet, nor the curtains at his back, but those to which his face was addressed. The curtains of his bed were drawn aside; and Scrooge, starting up into a half-recumbent attitude, found himself face to face with the unearthly visitor who drew them: as close to it as I am now to you, and I am standing in the spirit at your elbow. It was a strange figure – like a child: yet not so like a child as like an old man, viewed through some supernatural medium, which gave him the appearance of having receded from the view, and being diminished to a child's proportions."

-Charles Dickens, *A Christmas Carol*

Chapter One

Ghost of Christmas Past

MADDY MADISON couldn't have been happier that Christmas. This was the year her daughter Tilly had given birth to a beautiful little girl who'd been named Agnes in honor of her grandmother. Madelyn Agnes Madison had been flattered. True, Mark and Tilly Tidemore had compromised by adding a middle name that remembered Mark's long-deceased mother, Millicent – but that was only fair.

Being it was Christmas Eve, Maddy and Beauregard had invited their closest friends over for eggnog. Maddy always enhanced the recipe with nutmeg and whipped cream and just a dash of Captain Morgan's Spicy Rum. The rum was her secret ingredient. The eggnog (along with her decorated watermelon cookies) was a popular holiday staple.

Maddy kept a high-octane version in the back of the refrigerator, a concoction containing double the rum. That was Beau's favorite.

The four wives belonged to a quilting bee that they fancifully called the Quilters Club. Originally there had been more than a dozen members, but the group had dwindled down to this quartet: Bootsie, married to Caruthers Corner's Police Chief Jim Purdue; Cookie, wife of a local farmer named Bob Brown; Lizzie, the ostentatious wife of banker Edgar Ridenour; and Beau's clever wife

Maddy.

This year they also hosted Leslie Ann Holmes, a fifteen-year-old "exchange student" from London. Part of the Hands Across the Sea program. Maddy loved the girl's crisp British accent and Mary Poppins "spoonful of sugar" attitude.

Tilly and Mark would be dropping by later with Baby Agnes. Maddy wished Tilly's brothers and their wives could have made it home for Christmas. It was too long a drive for Freddie, a fireman in Atlanta. And do-gooder Bill was wrapped up serving plates piled with roast turkey to the needy in Chicago.

At the time Tilly and Mark were living in a cute little starter home on the outskirts of Caruthers Corners, a cozy bungalow befitting a young attorney fresh out of Harvard Law.

Mark was a junior member of Dingley & Bratts PC, a well-respected law firm in this part of Indiana. Bartholomew Dingley had been at it for over half a century, earning himself a reputation as a fair and honest litigator. Being a local boy, Mark had worked as a gofer at Dingley & Bratts during his high school years. In return, Bartholomew had written him a glowing letter of recommendation to Harvard, his own alma mater.

"Hark! The Herald Angels Sing" was playing loudly on the stereo, an old rendition by Fred Waring and his Pennsylvanians. Beau was a traditionalist at heart, fond of Big Band music and Kate Smith and Sing Along With Mitch. Maddy preferred crooners like Bing Crosby doing "White Christmas" or Johnny Mathis singing about "chestnuts roasting on an open fire."

Maddy always loved having a white Christmas. Matter of fact, it *was* snowing outside. This was the year of the big blizzard, but that bad weather was still days away. Tonight, big fluffy snowflakes drifted down like the inside of one of those shiny glass globes that featured a miniature snowman. But so far there was not enough snow outside to build a snowman.

Over in the square that faced the Town Hall, a chorale from St. Paul's United Methodist Church was singing "Silent Night" – you could have heard them from the Madison's Victorian on Melon Pickers Lane if Fred Waring hadn't been turned up so loud.

Maddy's husband was just about to make his annual toast to "Peace on Earth," a cup of eggnog hoisted into the air, when the telephone rang.

The plaintive *ring-g-g-g!* broke the festive mood. Being closest, Maddy reached for it.

"Razzlefrazzit!" muttered Beau, obviously aggravated by this electronic intrusion. He liked giving the toast. All those years in the Caruthers Corners Toastmasters Club counted for something, didn't it?

"Yes? Oh, just a moment," Maddy said, turning toward the police chief. "Jim, it's for you."

Jim Purdue took the receiver, the coiled line stretching across the punchbowl on the kitchen table, so taut it made a series of cursive loops. "Yep, whatzup?" he growled, his on-the-job voice. As he listened, you could see his brow wrinkle, the shiny dome unbroken by a hairline. "Okay, okay. I'm on my way."

"What is it?" asked Maddy as he handed the phone back to her to hang up. She was always the more curious one in their group.

"Gotta go. Seems ol' Sam Buttersworth is dead."

"Oh no," said Beau. "Sam came into the hardware store just yesterday. Bought some lights for his tree. He always waits till the last minute, decorating the tree at midnight on Christmas Eve. A family tradition."

"Poor Emmy, she'll be lost without Sam," said Cookie.

"Sam was such a nice man," added Lizzie. "Always holding open the door for you. A true gentleman."

"What happened?" asked Edgar. "Did he choke on a Christmas cookie?"

The police chief frowned. "No, that's the odd thing. Witnesses say he got run over by a reindeer."

Chapter Two

Dan's Den of Antiquity

THAT NIGHT Caruthers Corners looked like one of those miniature villages you see atop white cotton on a Christmas mantle. Snow covered the town's yards and sidewalks, dusted the roofs. Floats for the Christmas Parade clogged Main Street. Crowds lined both sides of the wide boulevard to watch Santa make his yearly appearance.

The tiny Midwestern town (pop. 2,976) enjoyed holidays, particularly Christmas Eve with its annual parade. Maybe a dozen floats, the high school marching band, the town's only fire truck, a juggling club, Barry Brown on his unicycle, the Straw Hatters, and, of course, Santa's float – all led by the mayor in his big red Caddy.

Strings of colored lights decorated the houses. The town square featured a giant Christmas tree with a blinking silver star on top. Town Hall was flanked by tall red-and-white-striped candy canes.

Cozy Café remained open, as did the Family Dollar Store. A few lonely souls were partaking of the diner's holiday dinner – turkey and stuffing and jellied cranberry sauce for only $9.95. Farther down Main Street squealing children dragged their parents into the Family Dollar, a low-priced emporium that stocked lots of toys this time of year. A few buildings down, Dan's Den of Antiquity had its lights on, but the cluttered interior hosted no shoppers. Dan Sokolowski had enjoyed most of his seasonal sales earlier in the week, antiques not being a last-minute purchase.

Sokolowski was an elderly man with a bushy white beard and a thick Eastern European accent. He was said to be an expert on Chippendale furniture, rare US coins, and paintings by Joseph Mallord William Turner. He bought and sold used Rolex watches, did a good business in second-hand jewelry, offered a wide selection of antique clocks. Rumor had it that he was a Holocaust survivor, but he always wore long-sleeved shirts making it difficult to check for numbered tattoos.

The bell over the door made Dan Sokolowski look up from his newspaper, today's *Burpyville Gazette*. Burpyville was the next town over, on the way to Indianapolis. He was surprised to see Mayor Henry Caruthers. That ol' weasel always rode in the lead car of the Christmas Parade. Sokolowski glanced at a clock (there were dozens on display), noting that it was 8:15. The Parade ought to be turning the corner just past Town Hall about now. So what was the Mayor doing here in his shop at this hour on Christmas Eve?

"Need to use your phone," barked Mayor Caruthers. He appeared to be agitated, but that was a common state of composure for the skinny little politician.

"Help yourself," Dan Sokolowski nodded toward the black dial instrument on the shop's counter. "Why are you not in the Parade?"

"Forget the dadburned Parade," the Mayor snapped. "It just got canceled."

"Cancelled? Who by?"

"Me. I'm the mayor, ain't I? I've got the authority to do that. Especially when we got a dead body blocking the route up Main Street."

Sokolowski took a deep breath. "Dead body?"

"Sam Buttersworth," said the Mayor as he dialed the phone. Placing that call to Police Chief Purdue. One of the deputies said the Chief was over at Beau Madison's house partaking of holiday cheer. Maddy's eggnog was known far and wide.

Dan Sokolowski frowned. "Sam's dead? He was in here only an hour ago. Made the strangest purchase."

"Hold on a minute. I gotta get Chief Purdue over here to take charge of the crime scene. His deputies are useless. They don't know how to deal with a murder."

When the Mayor got off the telephone, Sokolowski persisted: "Murder? You mean Sam's death was not an accident?"

"Not hardly. Ol' Sam was marching with the Straw Hatters – that's the barbershop quartet he sings with. Them boys were lookin' all spiffy in their hats and striped vests. They were walking in front of the Santa Claus float, the one that depicts Saint Nick in his sleigh pulled by eight reindeers. Harley Bradshaw was driving the tractor pulling it. Then all of a sudden, Harley speeded up and swerved to the left, running over Sam as deliberately as a trucker turning a 'possum into road kill."

"Do tell. Are the deputies holding Harley till Chief Purdue gets there?"

"That's the problem. Harley just kept on going. Turned the float left onto Second Avenue and skedaddled. Swung around so fast Fatty Johnson tumbled out of the sleigh onto the sidewalk. Might've been hurt 'cept for all that Santa Claus padding. Last we saw of Harley, he was heading toward Highway 21 Bypass, all the Santa's elves hanging on for dear life."

"Santa's elves? That's Mrs. Grundy's fourth grade class."

"Yeah, guess we'll have to charge Harley with kidnapping too."

"Are the deputies giving chase?"

"The police car was in the Parade. Got stuck there when everything stopped to keep from running over Sam's body. That would've been adding insult to injury, if the floats and cars and marchers had just kept on going up Main Street with no-never-mind to Sam Buttersworth, don'tcha think?"

"I hope those poor kids are all right. It doesn't sound like Harley Bradshaw's in his right mind – running over Sam and driving off with Santa's float."

"Good point. We'll also need to charge Harley with Grand Theft Auto, stealing the float like that. The tractor pulling the float belongs to Bob Brown. He lets 'em use it every year. Fits in there between the plastic reindeer you can hardly see it."

"Poor Sam. Guess Emmy's not going to get to enjoy her Christmas present. I hate to see such a joyous season ruined."

"Joyous season?" frowned Mayor Caruthers. "I thought you was Jewish. Didn't you guys kill Christ?"

"Guilty as charged. But I have a soft spot for Saint Nicholas and his practice of gift-giving. Helps local businesses, mine included." He'd learned to ignore such bigoted remarks. The burden of being one of the Chosen People.

"So what was Emmy getting under the tree?" There was

a bowl of peppermint candy on the shop's counter. The Mayor popped one into his mouth, his back molars crunching down on it with the determination of a beaver gnawing down a birch.

"I doubt the Buttersworths' tree is up yet. They liked to decorate it at midnight, you know."

"Why wait? I like to get in the spirit early. The tree in the Town Hall's been up since the week after Thanksgiving."

"To each his own," shrugged the antiques dealer. "I may as well close up for the night. Nobody will be doing any last-minute shopping after this tragedy."

"The Parade didn't even make it the full length of Main Street," the Mayor grumbled. "Lots of disappointed kids."

"Not to mention Mrs. Grundy's fourth grade class. No telling where Harley Bradshaw has taken them. Surely he won't harm those innocent youngsters."

"Well, he squashed Sam Buttersworth like a bug. No telling what he's capable of."

"Didn't Harley live with his sister?"

"No, with his aunt. His daddy's sister. His folks got killed in a freak electrical storm thirtysome years ago."

"Oh, that's right," nodded Dan Sokolowski as he turned off the lights, ushered the mayor outside, and locked the store's front door behind them. "It was a big rainstorm. They were walking through the town square carrying an umbrella. And *Zap!* – like the wrath of God – they were reduced to crisps."

The two men turned to go in opposite directions. Sokolowski lived by himself on the west side of town. The Mayor had to get back up the street to where the Parade had stalled in order to meet Chief Purdue.

Henry Caruthers hesitated, then turned back toward the departing antiques dealer. "Wait!" he called after Sokolowski. "You didn't say what Sam got Emmy for Christmas."

The older man paused, as if thinking over his reply. "He was going to take her on a second honeymoon to the Bahamas. A cruise. So he'd bought a toy boat at the Family Dollar and wrapped it up with the Royal Caribbean tickets. He was going to put it under the tree tonight."

"How do you know about this?" The Mayor sucked at his back molars, a chuck of peppermint candy stuck between the teeth. It was distracting.

"I told you – Sam was in the shop this afternoon. He told me about it. He said they had been married forty years come January and he wanted to make it special. He was going to renew his vows, get married again on board by the ship's captain. He was an old romantic when it came to his wife."

The Mayor succeeded in dislodging the peppermint. "Well, goodnight to you. And Happy Honey-nookie."

"Hanukkah," Dan Sokolowski gently corrected him.

"Right, whatever." He took two more steps before turning again. "Hey, you said he bought something strange from you," the Mayor recalled Sokolowski's earlier remark. "What was it?"

"Well, I thought it was an unusual purchase for Christmas Eve. It was a matched pair of antique dueling pistols."

"Decorations for his family room, no doubt. It's a regular man cave."

"I don't think so. These were old cap-and-ball flintlocks. But he wanted me to reassure him they worked. Said it was time to even up old scores."

Chapter Three

A Pair of Dueling Pistols

"OLD SCORES? What d'you think he meant by that?" mused Police Chief Jim Purdue.

"Beats me," shrugged Mayor Caruthers. "You'll have to ask Dan Sokolowski about that. I only know what he said Sam told 'im."

"I won't bother him tonight. Sam's body is in the mortuary; them school children got safely dropped off in the Wal-Mart parking lot down towards Burpyville; and Harley Bradshaw has disappeared along with Santa's float. May as well let Dan have a peaceful night, as much is left of it."

The police chief and the mayor were standing on the steps of Town Hall, about twenty feet from the scene of the crime. Snow was still coming down, white flecks like goose down from a ripped pillow. The town square across the street was layered in white. A few ragtag members of the high school band were sitting under the shelter of the bandstand, playing a melancholy version of "Silent Night" on their shiny brass instruments.

"How does a twenty-foot float with a sleigh and eight plastic reindeer disappear?" grumbled Mayor Caruthers. "Ain't like 'The Night Before Christmas' where Rudolph the Red-Nosed Reindeer flies off into the sky with the sleigh."

"Those are two different stories," Chief Purdue pointed out. "'The Night Before Christmas' was a poem by Clement

Clark Moore. 'Rudolph the Red-Nosed Reindeer' was a song recorded by Gene Autry."

"The Singing Cowboy? What's he got to do with Christmas?"

Chief Purdue rolled his eyes. "Gene Autry sold 25-million records of 'Rudolph the Red-Nosed Reindeer'," he pointed out, even though explaining anything to the mayor was a lost cause. "Also he wrote the song 'Here Comes Santa Claus.'"

"I thought he just sang about 'Tumbling Tumbleweeds.'"

"Apparently Gene Autry liked Christmas. 'Frosty the Snowman' was another of his big hits."

The mayor shrugged, shaking off the spattering of snowflakes. "I used to watch his movies when I was a kid. We had a movie house here in Caruthers Corners back then. But the Rialto closed its doors in the '70s when the cost of popcorn got too high."

By now the Parade had dispersed, the floats and marchers and most members of the high school band going off in different directions. The majority of the townsfolk had gone home. Despite the tragedy, this was still Christmas Eve and people had presents to wrap and eggnog to drink.

"Gotta inform Emmy Buttersworth of Sam's death," sighed the police chief. "Heck of a way to be spending Christmas Eve."

~ ~ ~

At that very moment, the phone rang at the Tidemore house. Mark picked it up as they came in the door. He and Tilly had been over at her parents' house for eggnog. Little Agnes was hugging the stuffed dog that had been a Christmas present from Grammy and Grampy. She loved doggies, giggling at the sight of every stray pooch they encountered. Caruthers Corners was a dog-friendly town.

"Hello, Mark Tidemore here."

"You're the lawyer, right?" said the voice at the other end of the line.

"Yes. Who is this?"

There was a hesitation. "It's Harley Bradshaw. I think I'm gonna need your services."

~ ~ ~

Dan Sokolowski crawled into bed. He was saddened by the news of Sam Buttersworth's demise. And irked by Mayor Caruthers's anti-Semitic remarks. Nobody particularly liked the mayor, but he was descended from one of the town's founders so he managed to garner enough votes to keep him in office. This was his fourth or fifth term.

What he hadn't told the mayor was that the dueling pistols had a specific appeal to ol' Sam. They had once belonged to his great-great-grandfather, Sir Samuel Langston Buttersworth, a passenger on the wagon train that had stalled in 1829 on the very spot that became Caruthers Corners.

Sokolowski had turned up the Buttersworth connection to the dueling pistols when researching their provenance. He had bought them off Harley Bradshaw, who claimed his ancestor had bested Sir Samuel in a duel, thus coming into possession of said weapons. It had been a dispute over a horse, as Harley relayed the history. The antique dealer had contacted Sam Buttersworth right away, assured of a quick sale.

And right he was. He'd made $400 profit on those rusty old dueling pistols. A tidy sale for Christmas Eve.

Chapter Four

Hands Across the Sea

ᘻADDY PHONED the Quilters Club Members on Christmas morning to wish them good tidings. The four women were best-est of friends. She also wanted to brag about the turquoise necklace her husband Beau had given her as a present, a lovely piece of jewelry that would go perfectly with the blue dress she planned to wear to church services tonight.

Maybe it wasn't as expensive as the emerald ring Liz's hubby had given his wife last year, but that was to be expected. Edgar Ridenour was president of Caruthers Corners Savings and Loan; Beau Madison ran a modest hardware store.

Beauregard Hollingsworth Madison IV was descended from a town founder too. His forbearer, along with Jacob Caruthers and Ferdinand Jinks, had led the wagon train that got stranded in this stretch of northeastern Indiana.

A party of fur traders and hardy pioneers, the twenty-wagon caravan had mired in the outstretches of the Never Ending Swamp near the Wabash River. There they had been attacked by a band of Potawatomi led by Chief Winamac. After a fierce battle, Col. Madison had declared that they would settle here on the spot they had defended so bravely.

According to *A History of Caruthers Corners and Surrounding Environs* by Martin J. Caruthers: "*The brave Colonel then did drive a stake in the raw earth and state in*

17

a loude voice: 'We have won this land in a rite fair fight with the savage Red Indians and we will not give it back. Let us build our homes here and travel no more."

However, the new hamlet was named after Jacob Caruthers, that decided by a coin toss. Col. Beauregard Madison could have cared less. However, Ferdinand Jinks resented the slight to his dying day, having campaigned that the naming should have been rightfully in his honor as he was the caravan's wagon master.

In his history, Martin J. Caruthers wrote, *"Colonel Madison took the results of the toss masterly. The foul Jenks behaved badly, choosing his homesite far from the others. Caruthers Corners had a proper and dignified sound to it and everyone but Jenks applauded the euphonious selection."* But, of course, the author was the grandson of Jacob Abernathy Caruthers.

With his connection to the town's founding fathers, Beau Madison got a fair share of respect. He served on the Town Council. He was president of the Rotary. He was always one of the Grand Marshals at the annual Watermelon Days Festival. But to Maddy, he was simply Pooh Bear, the gangly man who had wooed her and won her their senior year in high school. They were married right after college.

The turquoise necklace had particular significance to Maddy. She was a champion of Native Americans. She thought it horrible how her ancestors had come in and took their land. Indiana had once been known as "Indian Territory."

She was ashamed that Gruesome Gorge – a local state park – had been the site of a large massacre of Potawatomi.

But there was no undoing the past. You had to live with historical mistakes and hope the current generation learned from its forbearers' bad behaviors.

In 1838, the Potawatomi had been relocated to designated areas west of the Mississippi under Andrew Jackson's Indian Removal Act. There are fewer than 8,000 Native Americans left in the state of Indiana today.

Maddy liked to show her support of indigenous peoples by wearing handmade Indian jewelry and collecting painted pottery. Her back porch looked like a potters shed, ceramic containers filled with an array of flowering plants and leafy shrubs.

Truth was, the turquoise jewelry had been crafted by Navaho artisans, inhabitants of the southwest rather than Indiana. But it was the thought that counted. Beau was supportive of his wife's causes. He didn't even complain about her weekly meetings with the Quilters Club, her support of the SPCA, or her participation in the Hands Across the Sea program. They were enjoying Leslie Ann Holmes's visit.

~ ~ ~

Leslie Ann Holmes was the fifteen-year-old British girl living with Maddy and Beau that year. They were her "second family" sponsors in an international program called Hands Across the Sea. Leslie Ann got to attend a US school, absorb the culture, and broaden her horizons. Kind of like being an exchange student, but there was no reciprocal exchange – a one-way educational program designed to strengthen the relationship with our friends in the UK.

Leslie Ann was a chipper young lady, a pint-sized

Pollyanna with big green eyes and short red hair. She was always smiling and humming bouncy tunes. She got to sleep in Tilly's old room. The program had no criteria other than she maintain a passing grade in school. Nonetheless, she helped Maddy around the house, volunteering to wash dishes or vacuum floors. Sometimes she babysat for little Agnes.

Maddy had taken the girl under her wing like a mother hen, teaching her to make watermelon pie, accompanying her on shopping trips to Indy, and introducing her to the Quilters Club. Lizzie took to her right away, both being redheads, and taught her how to cut up fat squares and properly stitch swatches of fabric together. Before you knew it, Leslie Ann was working on a quilt of her own.

~ ~ ~

When Maddy had Bootsie Purdue on the phone that morning, she asked if there had been any developments in the Sam Buttersworth case. Being the police chief's wife, Bootsie always had the inside scoop on such matters. Not that she was one to talk. But the members of the Quilters Club kept few secrets from each other. This ya-ya sisterhood had started in high school, continued steadfast throughout college, and lasted right up to today. Now middle-aged, if that's what you could call fifties these days, they were all happily married women with grown children. Little Agnes was Maddy's first grandchild, a precocious little cutie with cornflower-blonde hair and big blue eyes.

"Harley Bradshaw turned himself in this morning," Bootsie reported. "Jim was irked at having to get up on a cold Christmas morning and go receive a prisoner." Now that the Purdue children were out of the house, Jim liked to sleep in on holidays.

"I'm surprised Jim could get out of your driveway. The snow really came down last night," noted Maddy. With the phone cradled against her shoulder, she was looking out the kitchen window at an arctic landscape. Under the thick layer of snow you couldn't tell where the streets ended and the sidewalks began. It almost hurt the eyes to look at the bright white scenery framed by her kitchen window.

The town's snowplow wasn't out this morning because Darnell Watson didn't work on holidays. Union rules, he claimed, although it must have been a very small union since he was the only snowplower under contract with the town.

"Jim put chains on before leaving the garage," Bootsie explained. "He thinks the town police should be like the US Post Office. Y'know, 'Neither rain, sleet, snow or gloom of night ...'"

"Beau's building a fire in the fireplace. You couldn't get him to go out on a cold morning like this. The thermometer outside my window says it's below freezing. I can see the birdbath from here. It looks like a skating pond for wrens and thrushes."

Bootsie was not to be topped. "Branches are breaking off the willow tree in my front yard from the weight of the snow. And the power lines are sagging. I just hope the town doesn't lose electricity."

Maddy got back on subject. "Did Harley say why he ran over Sam Buttersworth with the Santa float?"

"Harley's not saying anything. He got lawyered up."

"You don't say," Maddy mumbled, nibbling on a slice of watermelon fruitcake. A prize-winning recipe from last year's Watermelon Days.

"I would've thought you already heard. His lawyer is your son-in-law Mark."

That caught Maddy off-guard. "Mark the Shark?" Tilly's husband had quite the reputation in the courtroom. "But he doesn't do murder cases. His specialty is tax law."

Bootsie snorted. "Well, you better let him know that. Jim said he was coming on like Perry Mason this morning, negotiating Harley Bradshaw's surrender as if he was handing over Machine Gun Kelly."

"If Mark is taking the case, Harley must be innocent," said Maddy, nibbling at the fruitcake, trying not to make it obvious that she was eating while talking.

"Innocent? There must've been five hundred witnesses to the crime. Main Street was lined with folks watching the Christmas Parade. Everybody saw Harley do it."

"Maybe his gas pedal stuck or something."

"Not likely. Cookie says there's been bad blood between the Bradshaws and the Buttersworths for generations."

"She should know," allowed Maddy. As secretary of the local Historical Society, Cookie Brown had traced the genealogy of practically everybody in Caruthers Corners.

"Something about a duel between their great-great grandfathers."

"A duel? Like between Aaron Burr and Alexander Hamilton?"

"You'll have to ask Cookie. I didn't get the details."

~ ~ ~

Maddy did exactly that: She phoned Cookie Brown next. Aside from the question about the Bradshaws and Buttersworths, it was a chance to crow about the beautiful turquoise necklace she'd found under the tree this morning.

"Oh, hi," Cookie greeted her. "I was just about to call you. Did you hear that your son-in-law's defending Harley Bradshaw?"

"Bootsie told me. She said there was some kind of feud between the Bradshaws and Buttersworth."

"Where have you been, girlfriend?" Cookie retorted. "Everybody knows there's been a riff between those two families going back to when Col. Beauregard Madison brought them here on the wagon train in 1829."

"I've never heard the story," said Maddy. She wasn't much of a history buff, but she could count on Cookie to fill in the gaps. Spending her days sorting through old news clippings and historical documents, Cookie assumed that everybody should be as interested in the town's past as she was.

"Back when those first settlers – Beau's great-great grandfather and the others – got stranded here on the banks of the Wabash, a fight broke out between Mordicai Bradshaw and Sir Samuel Buttersworth. It was an argument over a lame horse; the buyer wanted his money back. Words were exchanged, honor was challenged, and it ended with Sir Samuel getting shot dead by Mordicai. The two families have never spoken since."

"I can see why not."

"Are you sure you haven't heard that story? It's right there in Martin J. Caruthers' history." Everybody in the county had read the book. There were at least three copies in the town library, donated by Mayor Caruthers, old Martin's grandson.

"Beau's the one in the family who's obsessed over his

ancestors. He helped pay for that bronze bust of Col. Beauregard Madison that sits outside the meeting room in the Town Hall. Cost a pretty penny, if I may say so,"

Cookie sniffed disdainfully. "Not a very good likeness. It doesn't match the portrait by Matthew Brady."

"Who cares what he looked like? The old bugger's been dead nearly two centuries."

"Shame on you, Maddy Madison. That is your husband's heritage you're casting aspersions on."

"Heritage indeed. We're talking about a dirty old fur trapper who got a statue in the Town Hall because his wagon broke down here. If he'd been a better wheelwright, we might be living in California."

"Who wants to live in California?"

"Well, it's warmer out there," said Maddy, looking out at the thermometer mounted on the side of the house. 30°F, it read.

"*Tsk, tsk,*" Cookie clucked her tongue as a gentle reprimand. "Your husband gets a lot of adulation because of his great-great grandfather, bad wagon wheel or not. Beau ought to run for mayor."

"Maybe someday. But for now he's got a hardware store to manage."

"I hear rumors about a Home Depot coming in," the bespectacled blonde said. "If that happens, he might need a backup career. Besides, somebody needs to unseat that scoundrel we have. Henry Caruthers is a disgrace to his ancestors."

"From what I've read, old Jacob Caruthers was no prize himself. He led the raid on those poor Potawatomi Indians camped in Gruesome Gorge. According to Martin J.

Caruthers' history, he slaughtered women and children as well as warriors. That's the precious heritage that we share with our friends and neighbors."

"Remember, dear, the Taylors were on that wagon train too," Cookie referred to Maddy's family tree. The Taylors had occupied a big house facing the square, built by old Simon Taylor – Maddy's great-grandfather.

"Yes, I know. The shame of it."

"Did you know the original name for Gruesome Gorge was a Bodéwadmimwen word meaning 'Peaceful Meadows'? That's were your local church gets its name."

Maddy squinched up her nose. "Bodéwad-what?"

"Bodéwadmimwen. That's what the Potawatomi language is called. It's a Central Algonquian tongue similar to Ojibwe or Shawnee ... or Sauk."

"Sauk? Is that a tribe too?"

"Yes. But during the Black Hawk War of 1832 the Sauk were pretty much wiped out by General Edmund P. Gaines. They had crossed the Mississippi to reclaim tribal land in Western Indiana, but the settlers didn't want to give it back."

"I've heard of Chief Black Hawk," said Maddy, a tad miffed at being lectured to. Her friend Cookie had a habit of doing that on historical topics. She should have pursued a career as a college professor. But Maddy would have likely flunked the course.

"Yes, Black Hawk was the warrior chief who led the so-called British Band against the Americans. Later on he wrote an autobiography, one of the first published in the United States by an indigenous native."

"A memoir by an Indian chief – that sounds interesting."

"I've got a first edition here on my bookshelf. It's titled

– wait a minute, let me read it off – *Autobiography of Ma-Ka-Tai-Me-She-Kia-Kiak, or Black Hawk, Embracing the Traditions of Native American his Nation, Various Wars In Which He Has Been Engaged, and His Account of the Cause and General History of the Black Hawk War of 1832, His Surrender, and Travels Through the United States. Also Life, Death and Burial of the Old Chief, Together with a History of the Black Hawk War.*"

"Wow, that's a mouthful," said Maddy. "Can I borrow it?"

"Nope. Historical Society property. You have to read it in our Reading Room."

"You don't have a Reading Room."

"Do too. We converted the side porch. It has a comfortable leather armchair donated by Nattie Harmon and a pole lamp from the remodeling at the Senior Center."

"Okay, I'll come read it there. But not till Spring. That side porch isn't heated."

"We're hoping someone will donate an electric heater."

"Wait a minute. I called you at home. If that book can't be removed from the Historical Society, what's it doing there on your bookshelf?"

"The binding is loose. I was taking it over to Dan Sokolowski to have him repair it, but holiday shopping got in the way."

"Likely story. But never mind that. What did Bob get you for Christmas?" Maddy asked, a way of leading up to a description of her new turquoise necklace.

"An electric drill."

"For you?"

"Oh, Bob's been wanting one. I don't mind. Trouble is,

I bought him one too. Now we have two Black & Decker drills. Do you think Beau will let me return one of them?"

"Don't worry, I'm sure he will. Better still, swap it for something *you* want. A new mixer perhaps. Your old one has certainly seen better days."

"That's a good idea."

"I can't believe your husband gave you an electric drill."

"Bob means well. But the poor shmoo hasn't got a romantic bone in his body. Do you remember the time he took me to the Ponderosa Steak House on my birthday?"

"But you're a vegetarian –"

"Exactly."

Maddy switched gears. Now didn't seem to be the time to brag about her turquois necklace. "About that feud between the Bradhaws and Buttersworths, do you think that's why Harley ran over Sam with Santa's sleigh last night?"

"Can't think of any other reason. Everybody loved ol' Sam. That is, everybody 'cept Harley and his Aunt Gloria. They're the only two Bradshaws left since his parents got struck by lightning."

"If I had to pick a way to die, I think I'd chose lightning," replied Maddy, her honey-brown hair bobbing as she nodded. "It would be a fast way to go. You wouldn't feel a lick of pain."

"Not me. I'd pick death by chocolate."

"You and Bootsie."

"She's been on that new watermelon diet."

"Does it work?"

"No, of course not. Have you seen her in that green dress she bought on her last shopping trip to Indy? It makes her look like a ripe watermelon."

"Be kind," shushed Maddy. She functioned as the unofficial leader of the Quilters Club, and worked hard at keeping the peace among her friends.

Peace on Earth and Mercy Mild, wasn't that what those "Hark! The Herald" angels sang?

Chapter Five

A Gnat in the Bonnet

"THAT'S A VERY NICE necklace," cooed Liz Ridenour. The redhead could afford to be generous in her compliments – after all, her hubby had bought her a diamond tennis bracelet for Christmas. Not that Lizzie played tennis. She didn't do sports, nor any activity that made her sweat. Her makeup was thick and her lips a bright red to match her hair. She considered herself "a fashion plate."

Lizzie shopped at Nordstrom; Cookie at Target; Bootsie at T.J. Maxx; and Maddy at Marshalls. That pretty much summed them up, aside from an unbending bond of friendship and a mutual affection for quiltmaking.

Maddy had to admit that her turquoise jewelry looked modest in comparison to Lizzie's flashy bracelet. As president of the Savings and Loan, Edgar Ridenour was the biggest breadwinner among the four families. Jim was a public servant, drawing a stipend from the town. Bob was a farmer, an uncertain occupation dependent upon the weather. And Beau eked out a meek-but-steady income with his Ace Hardware franchise. Ol' Edgar could count on a healthy six-figure income plus a bonus.

Oldest among the husbands, Edgar would be coming upon retirement soon. He planned to spend his Golden Years fishing the Wabash in his aluminum flat-bottomed boat. He vowed never to wear a three-piece suit again. And he threatened to grow a beard.

Lizzie loved soap operas, content to be a stay-at-home wife. Every day from 10 a.m. to 2 p.m. she watched her "stories." Afternoons were devoted to hobbies, mainly quilting and needlecrafts. She was the best quilter among the group, an inborn knack. As long as she had her Quilters Club cronies, she had no complaints about her husband going fishing whenever he liked. As long as he didn't expect her to clean his catch. You could chip a nail doing that.

"I love your tennis bracelet," Maddy said as she examined it up close. Diamonds, diamonds everywhere. Easily a five-grand price tag.

"Thanks, sweetie," said Lizzie, holding out her arm to display her prize. This morning the two women had met at the Cozy Café for coffee, a quick break before starting preparations on their Christmas dinners. Lizzie would cook for just herself and her husband this year, their daughter away at college. Maddy and Beau would have a houseful with Leslie Ann, plus Tilly and Mark and baby Agnes. Empty nesters, Jim and Bootsie would join them too. Cookie and Bob would be eating with his sister's family.

Cozy Café was featuring pumpkin latté today. Topped with whipped cream and a touch of cinnamon, it was perfect for the season. Outside the small diner, Main Street was all but impassable with newly fallen snow. People hurried past on the sidewalk, scarves wrapped around their necks, head down against the wind. Maddy almost couldn't get there in her big four-wheel-drive Ford Explorer.

Maisie, the waitress who'd pulled the short straw for Christmas Day duty, had just brought over complimentary slices of fruitcake when Cookie Brown pushed through the diner's revolving door. Looking like an Eskimo in her padded L.L. Bean coat, she stomped on the Welcome mat to free clingy snow from her calf-high boots.

"Look what the cat drug in," Lizzie greeted their friend.

"Maisie, another latté please," Maddy placed an order for the newcomer. Her appearance was a pleasant surprise. They hadn't been expecting to see Cookie today. Everybody was too harried, preparing big Christmas dinners.

"Hi all," said the thin blonde woman. She eyed the plates. "May I have a slice of that fruitcake too," she called to Maisie.

"What brings you out?" asked Maddy, taking a sip of the hot pumpkin latté.

"I called your house and Beau told me I'd find you two here. Bootsie will be joining us if she can get through the snowy streets. The town should fire Darnell Watson if he can't plow the streets when we need it."

Just then the door bust open again and a plump woman with dark pixyish hair appeared. "I'll have a latté and two slices of whatever they're having," announced Bootsie Purdue.

"Coming right up," responded Maisie from behind the counter. Stretching from one end of the dining car to the other, the stainless steel counter was measured by clusters of salt and pepper shakers, ketchup bottles, and frosted-glass sugar containers. However, Maddy and her friends always took the corner booth. More room to spread out.

"Well, well, the gang's all here," said Lizzie, leaving her hand on the tabletop where everyone could see her diamond bracelet. "Should we call the Quilters Club to order?"

While the tiny quilting bee had no formal rules, Maddy

solemnly replied, "Consider us now in session. What's going on, you two? Bootsie looks like she's got a bee in her bonnet."

"Maybe not a bee. More like a gnat," Bootsie grinned.

"Go ahead, let it out," urged Lizzie. She loved juicy gossip and insider info. And she knew the police chief's wife usually had both. "Did Mayor Caruthers get caught diddling his secretary?" In this part of the country personal assistants were still called secretaries and flight attendants were known as stews. UnPC perhaps, but old habits fade slowly.

"Ha! That's old news." Everybody knew about the mayor and Nancy Ann Beanie – that is, everybody except Nancy's husband Jasper.

"Must be something good to bring you out in this snow," commented Maddy.

"Okay, here's what I've got," whispered Bootsie, waiting until Maisie placed the coffee and fruitcake in front of her. The waitress was obviously curious but she knew continued patronage depended on privacy. As she drifted back toward the kitchen, Bootsie continued with a conspiratorial wink: "The Quilters Club has a mystery to solve."

"What kind of mystery?" said Lizzie, sounding dubious.

Bootsie smiled triumphantly. "It has to do with the death of Sam Buttersworth, of course."

Chapter Six

The Feud

"THERE'S NO MYSTERY there," Maddy said with a sigh. "Sam was killed by Harley Bradshaw. Half the town witnessed it."

"Yes, but the question is why?" countered Bootsie.

"Because of bad blood between them," said Cookie. "Everybody knows that. Goes back to when Harley's great-great grandfather shot Sir Samuel Langston Buttersworth in a duel over a lame horse. It's all there in Martin Caruthers's history book."

"And how did Harley's great-great grandfather shoot Sir Samuel?" Bootsie persisted.

"With a pistol, of course," snapped Cookie, exasperated by Bootsie's silly questions. "How else do you shoot someone?"

Maddy perked up. "Was it one of those dueling pistols ol' Sam bought from Dan's Den of Antiquity last night?" she asked, catching onto the thread of Bootsie's questions.

"Exactly," smiled the police chief's wife. She touched her nose to indicate that Maddy was spot-on.

"What's the big mystery in that?" Lizzie wanted to know. She was a tad slow with logical thinking. Not the steel-trap mind of Maddy or the fact-hungry personality of Cookie.

"Bear with me," insisted Bootsie. "The question is, where are those rusty old dueling pistols now?"

Cookie shrugged. "I'd expect Sam took them home, a Christmas present to himself."

"What if I told you the pistols aren't there?"

"Did someone check out the presents under the tree?" suggested Lizzie, the original Material Girl. "He might have wrapped them up as a gift to himself at the same time he wrapped that toy boat with the tickets for the anniversary cruise he was giving Emmy."

"No," said Cookie, buying into Bootsie's scenario. "The Buttersworths didn't wrap their presents or put up their tree until Christmas Eve. A family tradition."

"Right," nodded Bootsie. "No tree, no presents, no pistols."

"So where are the dueling pistols?" asked Lizzie.

"That's the mystery," Bootsie said. "The pistols are missing."

~ ~ ~

Being Jewish, Dan Sokolowski had nothing better to do than go down to his shop on Christmas day. His wife had passed a few years ago; their only child was living in New York City, a successful diamond merchant on 47th Street; and he had no one to celebrate Hanukkah with. So he figured he may as well work on that broken grandfather clock. No one would buy a clock that didn't tick.

Dan Sokolowski was trudging through the six inches of snow on the sidewalk when the door to Cozy Café burst open and he found himself surrounded by four chattering women. He recognized them – the police chief's pudgy hausfrau, the banker's redheaded spouse, that mousy woman who ran the historical Society, and the pleasant wife of the man who owned the hardware store down the street.

He knew them all by name, but he didn't normally socialize with townsfolk. He was a very private man.

"Whoa, whoa, don't all speak at once, ladies," Sokolowski tried to calm them down. "One at a time. I have but two ears."

The women looked at each other and made the unspoken consent that Maddy go first. She was a natural leader, the take-charge type.

Maddy cleared her throat, frosty breath hanging in front of her face like ectoplasm. "Mr. Sokolowski –" she began.

"Call me Dan," the antiques dealer interrupted. "It is short for Daniel. Like the man who faced a lion in the Old Testament." The reference was obvious: That he was confronting this pride of lionesses on snowy Main Street.

"Dan then," Maddy started over. "We have a couple of questions related to Sam Buttersworth."

"Ah, Sam. What a tragedy. He was in my shop just before the Parade last night."

"What time was that?"

"I would say about 7:30."

"The Parade started at 8:00," observed Maddy. "That means Sam didn't have time to go home. He lives all way out on Highway 21, near the turnoff for Gruesome Gorge State Park."

"Lived," Cookie corrected. Always a stickler for facts.

"Lived," Maddy acknowledged the proper tense.

"My husband said those were the very same pistols used in the duel between his and Harley Bradshaw's great-great grandfathers," Bootsie added.

"That is correct. The moment I acquired them, I phoned

Sam to ask if he would like to purchase them. That's what I do, buy and sell."

"Yes, but how did you know these were Sir Samuel Buttersworth's pistols?" queried Cookie, eager to establish the guns' historical provenance.

"Simple. The seller was Harley Bradshaw. He said the guns have been in his family ever since that fateful duel. And then I consulted Martin J. Caruthers's history. I keep a copy in my shop."

"Harley sold you the dueling pistols and you sold them back to the Buttersworth family," repeated Lizzie. "Sounds kinda grotesque."

"Mine is not to judge," Dan Sokolowski spread his hands in a what's-a-man-to-do gesture. He was wearing knitted mittens with a snowflake design. "I said it was strange."

"Why did Harley decide to sell these heirlooms after all these years."

"He didn't say. But Harley and his Aunt Gloria are the only remaining members of the Bradshaw clan. I assumed they had lost interest in this long-ago event and any artifacts associated with it."

"If Harley had lost interest in it, why did the feud between the two families still exist?" Cookie challenged.

Dan Sokolowski shrugged. "Some people have a natural dislike for each other. It doesn't have to be handed down through the generations."

"Maybe so," said Maddy. "But is it merely a coincidence that Harley Bradshaw killed Sam Buttersworth the same afternoon he purchased those dueling pistols?"

"Who am I to say?" replied Sokolowski. "But I am

freezing my kiester off out here on the sidewalk. If you ladies have more questions, you'll have to follow me down to my shop where it's warmer."

Without further words, the four members of the Quilters Club trailed behind the old man like ducklings heading to a pond.

Part 2

The Second of the Three Spirits

"Awaking in the middle of a prodigiously tough snore, and sitting up in bed to get his thoughts together, Scrooge had no occasion to be told that the bell was again upon the stroke of One. He felt that he was restored to consciousness in the right nick of time, for the especial purpose of holding a conference with the second messenger dispatched to him through Jacob Marley's intervention. But, finding that he turned uncomfortably cold when he began to wonder which of his curtains this new specter would draw back, he put them every one aside with his own hands; and lying down again, established a sharp look-out all round the bed. For he wished to challenge the Spirit on the moment of its appearance, and did not wish to be taken by surprise, and made nervous."

- Charles Dickens, *A Christmas Carol*

Chapter Seven

The Long-Lost Brother

BEAUREGARD NEVER talked about his older brother. Mycroft Madison was the black sheep of the family. They hadn't spoken in thirty years. That's why he was surprised by the phone call.

"Who?" Beau said into the phone. "Did you say Mikey?"

"That's right, you nimrod. Your brother Mikey."

Beau stared at the phone as if he could see the person on the other end of the line. Could it really be his brother? "Are you all right? Did anything happen?"

"I'm right as rain. Still here in New York. But not for long. Just bought into a retirement village in Ft. Lauderdale. That's in Florida."

"I know where Ft. Lauderdale is," Beau replied testily.

"You should come visit."

Visit? After thirty years without a single phone call? Not even a Christmas card, Beau thought to himself as he surveyed the colorful holiday greetings lining the mantle. "Er, yeah, sure. I look forward to it," he said, not meaning a word of it.

"You're probably wondering why I'm calling, right?"

"I've gotta admit it occurred to me. We haven't talked in quite a while."

"Sorry about that," said the voice. "Guess I was trying to put Caruthers Corners and everything connected with it behind me. You'll remember I had a big blowup with Mom

41

and Dad when I left."

"Do I. They're both gone now. I sent you a telegram about the funeral." Their parents had passed away more than twenty years ago, a car accident.

"Tell you the truth, I regret not coming. But it's hard confronting your past. Ebenezer Scrooge discovered that in *A Christmas Carol*."

"Well, this is not a Charles Dickens story. It's real life."

"Beau, you were always the responsible brother. Me, I've pursued my dreams. I had a great run as a theater director here in New York. Off Broadway mostly. But I've strutted and fretted my hour upon the stage. Time to turn off the footlights and join that retirement community in Ft. Lauderdale. After all, I'm a couple years older than you."

"Have a happy retirement, Mikey. I truly mean that."

There was a pause. "I'm sure you do. I'm sorry about that blowup with Mom and Dad when I left home. But I wasn't meant for small-town life. You were. Tradition and heritage were important to you. That's why I'm calling."

~ ~ ~

"I'm not sure I understand," Beau Madison said. Talking on the phone with his brother Mikey for the first time in thirty years took him by surprise. While his wife was having coffee with Cookie Brown, he'd been waiting for the snow to stop so he could shovel the walk. But it gave no sign of letting up.

"Do you remember that Christmas quilt we had when we were kids?"

Beau's mind wandered back to his childhood. Yes, there *was* a special quilt that featured a hand-stitched Santa Claus. He and Mycroft got to sleep under it on Christmas

Eve. "Yes, I do. Whatever happened to that old quilt?"

"I have it. Took it as a memento when I left home."

"We were grown men when you left."

"Guess that's why you didn't miss it. By then you were married to Maddy, sleeping in your own home."

Beau couldn't help but smile at the thought. Sleeping under that quilt had been a once-a-year treat for the two boys. He remembered every stitch in those patchwork squares. "I hope you've enjoyed it. You and I spent many a Christmas under that quilt."

"Indeed I have. My kids enjoyed the same Christmas treat we did. But they are both grown now."

"You have children?"

"Two boys. One's a lawyer in DC. The other a stockbroker here in New York."

"I'm sorry Maddy and I never got to met them."

"Me too. If I had it to do over —"

Beau didn't want to prolong the conversation. Too painful. "Water under the bridge," he said magnanimously. "Thanks for touching base. I'm sure you'll like the warmer weather of Ft. Lauderdale."

"No doubt. New York is pretty cold right now. Can't say I'll miss it. And according to the Weather Channel the temperature's well below freezing in Indiana."

"I can see the thermometer outside the window. It says 20 degrees ... although it's pretty hard to read the dial through all the snow."

"It's snowing, huh?"

"They say it's gonna be a heckuva blizzard."

"Then you're going to need a quilt."

"I don't understand?"

"I'm moving to smaller digs in Florida. That means I've got to get rid of a lot of stuff. My kids don't want the Christmas quilt. They saw it as a childhood pleasure, but they're not sentimental. I suspect you are."

"You mean you're giving me the Christmas quilt?"

"If you want it."

"I'd be honored to have it. I always loved that old quilt."

"Then I'll ship to you overnight. Didn't make Christmas Eve, but you'll still have it for the holiday season."

"Mikey, I'm very grateful."

"Take it as an apology for being so slow to get in touch."

"Hey, an apology will take more than a ratty old quilt."

"Oh?"

"It'll take a visit from you one of these days. We'd love to see you."

"It's a deal. After I get settled into the retirement village."

"Well, goodbye. And have a Merry Christmas."

"One more thing"

"What's that?"

"Back when I took the quilt with me I found something."

"What —?"

"When I unfolded the quilt, a slip of paper fell out. It was an invoice. Turns out, our mom didn't make that quilt; she got it from our great-grandmother."

"She made it?"

"No, according to the invoice she bought it."

"From whom?"

"That's the interesting part."

Chapter Eight

The Mayor's Day Off

MAYOR HENRY CARUTHERS had arranged to meet his secretary at their office in the Town Hall. This was Christmas Day and the building was closed, but they each had keys. They had been carrying on behind her husband's back for years.

Nancy Ann Beanie was married to the town ne'er-do-well. They had no fear of being caught by her husband today. Jasper Beanie was sleeping it off in the holding cell at the police department. He occupied that cell so often, the police had dubbed it "Jasper's Second Home."

The affair between the mayor and his assistant was an open secret. Most people felt Jasper Beanie deserved the cuckolding. He was a nasty, unkempt little man, beloved by none. He worked as the caretaker for Pleasant Glade, the large cemetery on the edge of town. He and his wife lived in the caretaker's cottage near the front gate. The structure was pretty rundown – sagging roof, loose siding, a hinge broken on the back door – belying the term "caretaker."

Today the mayor and Nancy Ann were exchanging Christmas presents while sharing a glass of sparkling wine he'd bought at the Food Lion for this occasion. He hoped to top it off with some hot action in the meeting room. If the Town Council knew what despicable acts had taken place on the conference table, they'd never lay their papers on its polished surface again.

Nancy Ann was just hiking up her skirt when they heard the front door of the Town Hall bang open. At first the mayor thought he might not have properly closed the door and it had been blown open by a gust of wind. The snowstorm was still raging outside – 30 MPH winds, according to the radio.

When he heard footsteps coming up the steps, he figured the Tax Collector might be coming back because he'd forgotten his briefcase. Showing touches of early Alzheimer's, the man was always forgetting something. The Town Council would have to replace him soon.

"You stay in here and keep quiet," whispered the mayor. "I'll go get rid of whoever it is."

"Just hurry. I have to be home before Jasper gets there. The cops usually release him around noon."

"We got plenty of time," the spindly man said, glancing at his watch. "It's barely 11 a.m." Their trysts were usually brief for Henry Caruthers suffered from ED problems, like those you see Bob Dole talking about on TV.

"Hello," came the voice from downstairs. "Henry, are you here?"

"Who's that?" the mayor returned the call, hastily buttoning his trousers.

"It's Jim Purdue. I saw your car in the back lot. Need to ask you a question or two concerning Sam Buttersworth's death."

"Be right down. But you'd get better answers from Doc Medford." A local physician doubled as county coroner.

"Already talked to him this morning," the voice replied. "He'll have his findings in a couple of days."

"So wait."

"Gotta investigate the crime while it's hot," said the police chief. "Helluva way to spend Christmas."

"A better day for you than for ol' Sam," Henry Caruthers pointed out, suddenly appearing at the foot of the stairwell. His shirttail was hanging out. Chief Purdue made no mention that he'd spotted Nancy Ann Jasper's clunky old Plymouth parked in the back lot also.

Jim Purdue didn't care who the mayor was diddling. But you'd think he could be smarter about it. Problem was, brains didn't run in the Caruthers bloodline. "Wanted to make sure I understood what Dan Sokolowski said to you last night."

"Why don't you ask him? I'm piled high with paperwork. That's why I came in today."

Yeah, sure. "I *will* ask him, but you know how police work goes. You question all the witnesses."

"Then you've got a big task ahead of you. Must've been five hundred people who saw Harley run over Sam Buttersworth. Fatty Johnson is threatening to sue the town for injuries sustained when he fell outta the sleigh. Says he won't be playing Santa Claus next year. Kids are sure going to be disappointed."

"We'll get Bob Brown to play Santa. He won't need any padding." Cookie's husband weighed in at 300 pounds. Add a fake beard and red suit, you'd have a serviceable Kris Kringle.

"What about Fatty's lawsuit?"

The police chief sighed. "He's just talking. I'll calm him down. Worst comes to worst, we'll pay his doctor bills."

"So what questions do you have for me?" asked Mayor Caruthers, glancing nervously toward the stairwell. He hoped Nancy Ann would heed his advice and stay in the meeting room. She was a headstrong woman. Everybody knew she ran the mayor's office, more in charge of the town's operations than Henry Caruthers. He barely qualified as a figurehead.

"You said Dan Sokolowski referred to it as an 'unusual purchase'. What was so unusual about Sam buying back a family heirloom?"

The mayor shrugged, getting fidgety. "Beats me. Like I said, you'll have to ask Dan Sokolowski. I'm not a mind reader."

"I though maybe he'd said more."

"He said Sam mentioned 'evening a score.'"

"With Harley Bradshaw?"

"Don't ask me. You got the murderer locked up in the cell next to Jasper Beanie. Case closed as far as I'm concerned. Ain't no doubt of Harley's guilt, all them witnesses who were lined up to watch the Christmas parade. Who gives a fig about those dadburned guns?"

~ ~ ~

Apparently, the Quilters Club gave a fig. The four women huddled around Dan Sokolowski's kerosene stove, warming their hands and brushing snow off their coats. Lizzie's coat was real fur, even though her friends frowned on that. But Lizzie liked to show off that her husband could afford to buy her a mink. Never mind those poor little weasel-like donors.

"So what else do you want to know?" prompted the proprietor. He'd rather be fixing that grandfather clock than chatting with them. He'd always been uncomfortable around women.

Before they could answer, the bell over the door jingled like Santa's sleigh and Police Chief Jim Purdue walked in. He took about two steps before stopping dead in his tracks, staring at the Quilters Club. "Bootsie, what are you gals doing here."

"This is a public place," she replied testily. "Maybe we're shopping for antiques."

"Likely story," he huffed. "You nosy-Parkers are poking around in police business again. Go home and let me handle this. I'll meet you at Maddy's for Christmas dinner."

"Go ahead and do your police business," said his wife. "We'll just look around at the clocks. We need a new grandfather clock for the hallway." She patted a nearby clock's six-foot-tall oak cabinet as if admiring it.

"That clock does not work," warned Dan Sokolowski. "I was coming in today to fix it."

Jim Purdue could see himself having to shell out six grand for an antique clock when a $300 replica from Wal-Mart would tell time just as well. "Okay, you gals can stay, but leave the questions to me. Maddy, this is going to cost you an extra serving of turkey when we come over for dinner this afternoon."

"You would have gotten one anyway," she replied. "But we promise to keep quiet." She made a zipping motion across her lips.

Chief Purdue turned to the antiques dealer. "Dan, I wanted to confirm that Sam Buttersworth left the shop with those dueling pistols in hand yesterday. He didn't leave them here to pick up later by any chance?"

"Why do you ask that?"

"Well, we can't find them guns anywhere. Not at his

A Christmas Quilt

house. Not at the high school where his barbershop quartet gathered before the Parade. Nowhere we can think of to look."

Sokolowski appeared thoughtful, rubbing his bushy gray beard as if it might conjure up an answer. But not so. "Sorry, I can't help you on that. Sam walked out of the store carrying the gun case in a brown shopping bag."

"Case?"

"That's right. The two dueling pistols were in a black walnut case trimmed with ivory. A lovely piece. I'd cleaned most of the rust off the guns. They hadn't been well cared for, no regular oiling or anything. One of them was badly damaged."

"Damaged?"

"Like it had exploded. Flintlocks were notoriously unreliable."

"Henry Caruthers said you called it an 'unusual purchase.' Why would you describe it that way? After all, it was a pair of historic pistols that had belonged to Sam's great-great grandfather."

"Buying guns on Christmas Eve is a little unusual, in my experience," replied the antiques dealer. "Usually people are thinking Peace On Earth on that day."

"But as I understand it, you called him and offered to sell the guns."

"True, but he insisted on coming down right away to collect them. Wanted to make sure I'd be open late enough on Christmas Eve for him to get here in time."

"In time to buy them on Christmas Eve ... or before the Parade."

"Both I suppose. All I can say is he seemed awfully

50

anxious to get them right away."

"Afraid you'd sell them to someone else?"

"No, he said he'd take them the minute I called. Agreed to my price without bargaining. Took me aback, in that I would have been willing to come down by a hundred dollars or more. I like to haggle. It's like a sport."

"So that's why you thought this an 'unusual purchase,' him eager to get the guns on Christmas Eve?"

"That and what he said about them."

Chief Purdue looked puzzled. "Said about them?"

"Wanted to know if they worked. He said he wanted to settle an old score."

"But Harley Bradshaw killed him, not vice versa," blurted Maddy, breaking her promise to keep quiet. Jim Purdue wasn't surprised, other than the fact she'd waited this long to butt in.

"If I'd thought anybody was going to be harmed, I never would have sold him the pistols," said Sokolowski. "And I would have reported the incident to Chief Purdue. It is not clear he was making a threat against Mr. Bradshaw or anyone else."

"But still you thought it a strange thing to say," prompted the Police Chief.

"A puzzling thing, would be a better way to put it."

~ ~ ~

The Quilters Club loved these types of challenges. Some people enjoyed solving crossword puzzles, others liked playing bridge, still others were addicted to pinochle. Maddy and her friends thrived on getting to the bottom of mysteries.

Their husbands didn't approve of this avocation,

especially Bootsie's. Chief Jim Purdue viewed them as benevolent meddlers. But if he were to be honest about it, he'd admit the four women were expert sleuths.

And they agreed with Dan Sokolowski that Sam Buttersworth's death was puzzling.

Chapter Nine

A Quiltmaker of Little Note

"HON, HAVE YOU ever heard of a woman named Sarah Soldemeir? She's probably long dead by now."

Maddy cocked her head, as if delving into some distant warehouse of memories. "Soldemeir – Sarah Soldemeir? Yes, she was a quiltmaker from the 1800s. A cousin of some famous cartoonist. Nothing special about her quilts. There was an article about her in *Quilting Monthly* last year."

"I think we may be getting one of her patchworks."

"Hm, why would we want that? Like I said, she was a dedicated quiltmaker but showed no outstanding talent."

"Apparently it's a family heirloom."

"Whose family?"

"The Madison clan. My brother is sending it to me."

"Mycroft? You've heard from him?"

"He phoned earlier today."

"Out of the blue?"

"Seems he's retiring and wanted me to have the quilt."

"Why would he have a Soldemeir?"

"He got it from our Mom. Question is, why would she have one?"

~ ~ ~

At fifteen, Leslie Ann was still shy around boys, not as precocious in that department as some of her American classmates. She hadn't even started wearing lipstick. Rumor was that a senior named Billy Hofstadter liked her, but he hadn't got around to asking her out. Maybe he'd get up his courage in time for the New Year's Father Time Dance, an annual event in Caruthers Corners.

The idea was Father Time ushering in the New Year, so the attendees were an eclectic mixture of older citizenry and the high school crowd. A gala affair, it was held in the high school gymnasium, that being the largest facility in town. The Tommy Tucker Band was playing this year. Their swing music was very danceable for the older folk.

Other than time spent with the Quilters Club, Leslie Ann led a rather solitary existence as a stranger in a new country. She had become friends with the Andrews sisters (no, not the old singing group, but rather Mary and Catherine Andrews, the twins whose family lived on Easy Chair Lane). The three girls sometimes met for milkshakes at the DQ, even though Maddy had showed them how to make snow cream, using a little vanilla syrup and milk mixed in a bowl with new-fallen snow. But at the DQ they got whipped cream and a maraschino cherry on top of their Rocky Road shakes. Delish, they agreed.

The Andrews sisters phoned to wish Leslie Ann a Merry Christmas. Santa had brought the twins matching cashmere sweaters. Father Christmas left a new dress for Leslie Ann. It would be perfect for the Father Time Dance. The girls agreed to get together and compare gifts when the snow let up.

Chapter Ten

Talking Turkey

CHRISTMAS DINNER at the Madison house on Melon Pickers Lane was rather glum. Jim Purdue was irked that his wife and her friends were meddling in police business. Beau shared the sentiment, not pleased that his wife and her Quilters Club gang were trying to play detective.

Baby Agnes was colicky, distracting her parents. Leslie Ann was helping out with the cranky child, but Agnes's unsettled nature reflected the mood of those seated around the table.

"Pass the cranberry sauce," said Jim Purdue, a clear sign he was unhappy. He usually preferred Maddy's watermelon sauce, a holiday tradition. Once the site of vast watermelon fields, the town was world famous for its annual Watermelon Days Festival. Elvis had once made an appearance early in his career. Being a Mississippi boy, he liked watermelon.

Lizzie handed over the bowl, it being closest to her. Besides, it was an opportunity for the banker's wife to flash her diamond tennis bracelet. Maddy was surprised the $5,212 price tag wasn't still dangling from its catch.

Being that so much of the day had been taken up with Sam Buttersworth's missing pistols, they had decided to consolidate Christmas dinner into a singular gathering – Madisons, Purdues, and Tidemores now joined by the

Ridenours and Browns. One big (un)happy family.

After all, the food preparation could be combined. And the Madison's large Victorian house was already decorated with lights and garland and mistletoe, conveying the proper holiday spirit. A Yule log burned in the fireplace. A gaudily decorated seven-foot-tall fake tree took up one corner of the living room. On the stereo Perry Como was crooning "Have Yourself a Merry Little Christmas."

Beau and Jim put the extra leaf in the dining room table and soon it was displaying a smorgasbord of turkey and all the trimmings – heaping bowls of creamy mashed potatoes, candied yams, and green beans, not to mention the pans of turkey stuffing, cranberry and watermelon sauces, and hot buns fresh from the oven. A brass coffee urn and pitchers of eggnog – spiked and unspiked – sat on the mahogany sideboard.

With all the hustle and bustle, dinner started a half-hour late but no one was complaining when faced with such a sumptuous feast. You'd almost expect the Ghost of Christmas Past to drop by as they waxed nostalgic over favorite Christmases of yesteryear. The time Maddy's son Freddie set the Christmas tree on fire. Or that time Tilly's dog stole the turkey. Or when Jim – just a beat cop then – arrested a burglar trying to steal the presents from under the Christmas tree at his very own home. Or when carolers in the town square changed the lyrics in "O Come, O Come, Emmanuel" into a bawdy tale worthy of Chaucer.

They had agreed not to discuss ol' Sam's death over dinner, but Maddy couldn't help herself. "What if Sam was planning on shooting Harley, but Harley heard about it and got him first?"

"That makes sense," nodded Cookie. Her husband rolled his eyes, knowing the dinner was about to go off track like a locomotive taking a curve too fast.

"I'll talk with his aunt tomorrow. See if she can shed any light on the matter," said Jim Purdue, trying to put the topic to rest. He wanted to eat his turkey leg in peace. It was well established that Jim got dibs on the turkey legs. And with three turkeys, he had plenty to fill his plate. Only the corpulent Bob Brown could keep up with Jim when it came to eating.

Bootsie came in third. Beau and Lizzie were picky eaters. Cookie was a vegetarian. Mark and Tilly had medium appetites like Maddy. Little Agnes was still on baby food, but they had broken out the Gerber's turkey flavor for the occasion. Leslie Ann picked at her food, probably wishing she had some Figgie pudding.

"Still, what happened to the dueling pistols?" continued Maddy, bugged by loose ends.

"They will turn up," Beau waved away her question to allow his friend Jim to eat without dyspepsia. "Sam probably gave them to someone to hold for him while he marched in the Parade."

"What will the Straw Hatters do without a fourth member?" posited Tilly, like her mother not taking the hint.

"Darnell Watson's got a good voice," volunteered Edgar Ridenour. "I heard him sing 'O Solo Mio' once. Made me nearly cry."

"Darnell Watson had best plow the streets tomorrow or we'll all be stuck in our homes, forced to live off leftover turkey," said Lizzie. You could tell she was not a fan of second-day sandwiches.

"Fine with me," laughed Bob Brown, a big jolly man. "Nothing I like better than leftover turkey unless it's cold pizza." You had the impression Bob would eat a rock if you put a little ketchup on it.

"I stock up with food for emergencies like that," said Cookie.

"Good idea," nodded Bootsie. "If you were holed up with Bob without food, it might turn into the Donner Party."

"Donner Party?" asked Leslie Ann, not familiar with American history.

"A group of early settlers who got stuck in the snow and wound up eating each other," Maddy explained.

"Hey, it's gonna come to that," said Mark Tidemore. "*Soylent Green* is our future if there are food shortages."

"That or insects," said Beau. "I read an article about it."

"Yuck, insects," Lizzie Ridenour made a face.

"Insects contain high protein," offered Leslie Ann. Making everyone wonder what the British ate. Grasshoppers and katydids covered in Hollandaise sauce?

"Don't worry, sweetie," Lizzie's hubby patted her hand. "You won't have to eat bugs. There are plenty of fish in the Wabash."

The redhead rolled her eyes. She refused to eat fish from the local river, no matter how many Edgar brought home from his weekend excursions.

"Maybe Sam gave the pistols to one of the wives of the Straw Hatters to hold until after the Parade," Maddy returned to the subject.

Jim Purdue didn't look up from his plate, bald dome gleaming in the light of the overhead chandelier. "I'll ask them tomorrow," he mumbled between gnaws on a turkey leg.

"We could call them for you," his wife volunteered. "They'd talk more freely with us than you, dear. Nobody likes to talk to the police. Except those of us at this table."

"Thanks," he said, not meaning it. "But I've got a deputy. Pete Hitzer's a good man. He'll check them out."

"Petie's a wonderful deputy," Cookie agreed. "His family came here from Switzerland two generations ago. Fine alpine stock. Bootsie's just suggesting we'd be happy to help out."

"Yes," said Lizzie. "Maybe you could deputize us. Make us official. Could we get badges? I think a badge would look good with my new tennis bracelet." She flaunted the diamonds on her wrist for all to see.

"Sorry, we're all outta badges," said the police chief. "I'm saving the last one for little Agnes."

Tilly beamed. "I'm sure Agnes will make a great detective when she grows up. Just like her Grammy."

"Thank you, dear," Maddy acknowledged the compliment. "We try to do our civic duty."

"Civic duty," snorted Beau, nearly spraying a mouthful of mashed potatoes onto his plate. "You just like to poke your nose into other people's business."

"Yeah, you gals best stick to your quiltmaking," nodded Jim Purdue, trying not to sound too harsh.

"I want to be deputized too," Leslie Ann spoke up. "After all, I'm an honorary member of the Quilters Club."

"Yes, dear, you are," Lizzie nodded. "Your quilt is coming along just fine. Nice tight stitching."

"You make it sound like the Quilters Club is a detective agency," laughed Bob Brown, a roly-poly man who saw humor in everything.

"Maybe we *should* be detectives," said Maddy. "And Leslie Ann can be one too."

"With her last name, she's probably a direct descendant of Sherlock Holmes," teased Bob.

"Sherlock Holmes was a fictional character," Cookie corrected her husband. "You can't be descended from someone an author made up."

"Arthur Conan Doyle based Sherlock Holmes on his old university professor Joseph Bell," offered the girl. "Dr. Bell was a third cousin twice removed on my mother's side. Does that count?"

"Impressive credentials indeed," beamed Maddy. "Detecting's in your DNA."

"What's a third cousin twice removed?" asked Bob Brown, confused.

"I'd think Emmy Buttersworth would be happy to have us recover the missing dueling pistols," Cookie continued, ignoring her husband's lack of genealogical enumeration. "After all, they're a treasured family heirloom, something for her to remember Sam by."

"Treasured family heirloom," scoffed Edgar. "The Buttersworth haven't had those dueling pistols in the family since Sir Samuel Langston Buttersworth got plugged between the eyes by one of those very same flintlocks. Not exactly what I'd consider pleasant memorabilia from the past."

Lizzie spoke up, "Dan Sokolowski said Sam paid him $1,400 for those pistols. That makes them valuable. I'll bet Mr. Sokolowski would take them back and refund the purchase price – or close to it. Who knows, maybe Emmy Buttersworth needs the money. I doubt ol' Sam was that well off."

"*Ahem,*" said Mark Tidemore. "I can't comment on this since Sam Buttersworth was a client. But I drew up his will last week. You don't have to worry about his wife."

Maddy looked up. "You didn't tell us about Sam making out a will."

"Client-attorney privilege," her son-in-law said. "I'm not allowed to talk about what I do for clients. I'd lose my license to practice law."

"I've always wondered why they call it practicing," said Lizzie. "Don't attorneys ever become good at it?"

"We try," smiled Mark the Shark. If you become a lawyer you've got to take the jokes.

"That's interesting," said the police chief. "About the will."

"What about the will?" said Mark.

"That he drew it up just a week before he died."

"Do you think there's a connection?" said Mark. "While I can't reveal details, I can say it was a pretty standard will, dividing everything between his wife and one other person."

"What other person?" asked Beau.

"Sorry, Dad. Can't say."

"If I thought it was relevant, I could get a subpoena that requires you to talk," said Jim Purdue. "That would let you off the hook with the Indiana Bar."

Mark thought about it for a moment, chewing on his turkey. "Maybe you'd better do that," he said at last.

Chapter Eleven

An Unwanted Gift

JASPER BEANIE sneaked around the unclipped shrubbery that hid the Buttersworth farmhouse from the main road. It was located only a half-mile from Gruesome Gorge, so ol' Sam wanted to have a privacy fence from all the tourists who passed by on their way to the state park. Aside from the park's history as the site of a long-ago Indian massacre, the scenic canyons offered waterfalls, swimming ponds, and a self-guided nature walk. In addition there were wooden picnic tables and barbeque grills and leveled-off campsites. A big draw for weekend visitors.

Sam and Emmy Buttersworth had shared this modest clapboard house ever since they got married following high school. There was a barn out back and forty acres of corn. Right now it was buried under snow. Jasper had to wear his knee-high snow boots to climb the hill leading up to the house. He practically needed a dog sled.

Jasper quietly placed the package on the front step, deliberating whether or not to ring the doorbell and run. Like a high-school prank, a way of signaling the package's presence on the snow-covered step. But since he couldn't move very fast in the snow, he decided to just leave it for Emmy to find in the morning.

The little man trudged back to his car, a rusty '98 Plymouth bellowing clouds of exhaust into the night air. He pulled a whisky bottle from his pocket, finished it off, and tossed the bottle aside. "Heaven help me," he muttered to himself, heart pounding like a jackhammer. "I'm not cut out to be a sneak thief." But as he reasoned it, he wasn't really a thief because he was merely leaving something on the Buttersworths' porch, not taking anything away.

In fact he was doing a good deed – no matter that he was being paid for it.

~ ~ ~

The day after Christmas is known to the British as Boxing Day, a day when wealthy landowners used to distribute boxes of leftover food to their serfs. In England it's counted as an official holiday, but Midwesterners simply go back to work.

Leslie Ann explained the tradition over breakfast. Just oatmeal this morning. That or turkey sandwiches was the choice. There was plenty of turkey left over from yesterday's Christmas dinner. More than enough to distribute to the town's needy, if it came to that.

"What a nice idea, giving leftover food to the poor," said Maddy. "Maybe we'll take a basket of goodies over to Emmy Buttersworth."

"Emmy's not poor anymore. Mark the Shark hinted that ol' Sam had a big insurance policy."

"Well, she hasn't collected any money yet," Maddy pointed out. "And she needs to eat *something* today."

"Oh goody," squealed Leslie Ann. "A mission of mercy."

~ ~ ~

Beau Madison opened the hardware store as usual, noting that the Family Dollar was already crowded with customers looking for After-Christmas sales. Bob Brown worked at the Wal-Mart down near Burpyville, only farming on the side. They would be having big sales too, all those 38" Samsung LCD televisions made in Korea and Dell D630 computers made in China. Edgar Ridenour was seated at his desk at the Savings and Loan, checking stock fluctuations on his clunky IBM desktop. Police Chief Jim Purdue was over at Judge Crammer's chambers, getting a subpoena that would compel Mark Tidemore to reveal the contents of Sam Buttersworth's will.

That gave the Quilters Club a head start in talking to the wives of the Straw Hatters, the barbershop quartet ol' Sam had been marching with when he got flattened by the Christmas float. Disappointingly, to a one, none of the wives had been asked to hold a brown paper bag containing the dueling pistols. And when each of them phoned their husband at work, at the urging of their visitors, none of them recalled seeing Sam with a package.

Puzzling. Those pistols had to be somewhere.

Chief Purdue was going to be angry that they'd beat him to these interviews, even though they'd turned up squat. Bootsie could handle him; a couple of nights sleeping in separate beds should do the trick.

~ ~ ~

Chief Purdue got the phone call from Emmy Buttersworth around noon. "You best get out here right away," she told him. "When I went out this morning to put more seed in the bird feeder, I found a package on my front step. It was a wooden case holding two old guns. I'd guess it's those dueling pistols Sam wasted his money on the day he died."

"Yes ma'am, I'm on my way."

Lights flashing, the police chief and his deputy were there within fifteen minutes. The snowy roads had little traffic, allowing them to make good time.

What aggravated him to no end was that Maddy Madison's big Ford Explorer pulled up behind his police cruiser no more than three minutes later. In it, he spotted the four members of the Quilters Club, including his wife Bootsie. What the blazes were they doing here?

"Hi, hon," called Bootsie. "We're just making a sympathy call on Emmy Buttersworth. Brought her some leftover turkey and a watermelon cake." She held up a cake platter as Exhibit A.

"It's a Boxing Day tradition," called Leslie Ann Holmes. He hadn't seen the girl, wedged into the backseat between Lizzie and Cookie. Hail! Hail! The gang's all here ... including the junior member.

"Boxing Day, huh?"

"That's right, dear. What are you and Pete doing out here?"

Jim Purdue knew his wife was shining him on, but there was nothing he could do about it. "Okay, be honest. How did you hear about the package on Emmy's doorstep?" he asked resignedly.

"I called your office and the new dispatcher said you were on your way out here. She was being nice to the boss's wife."

"You gals didn't waste any time."

"We were working on quilts at the Senior Center. That's half way here."

Pete Hitzer called out, "Chief, you better come look. I found footprints in the snow."

The prints were barely visible, filled up with layers of fresh snow. The tracks led down to a pull-off area near the mailbox.

"Looks like whoever delivered the package parked down here," Chief Purdue surmised.

His deputy nodded agreement. "Probably six or seven hours ago, judging by how much the snow has filled the tracks." He was an Assistant Scoutmaster with Troop 49 and knew how to read signs of nature.

"Who could it be?" asked Bootsie. "We talked to all the Straw Hatters and their wives this morning. None of them saw a package."

"You talked to –?" Chief Purdue was taken aback.

"Just helping out, dear."

"Bootsie, I told you –" But his words were interrupted by the excited voice of Maddy Madison.

"Over here," she called. "I think I've found a clue."

Everyone gathered around her, even Emmy Buttersworth. Maddy was pointing at an empty whisky bottle protruding from the snow. It was only a few feet from the tire tracks at the mailbox. Chief Purdue pulled out a ballpoint pen and inserted it into the lip of the bottle, gingerly lifting it out of the snow. The label on the glass surface proclaimed: Wild Boar.

"Looks like the visitor was fortifying himself against the cold," said Pete Hitzer.

"Or working up the courage to deliver the package in the dark of night," said Bootsie.

"Or maybe he was just a lush," suggested Lizzie. She nipped a bit on the side, nothing serious. But she understood the alcoholic habit.

"I recognize that brand," said Chief Purdue. "It's a cheap whisky that drunks favor, more for its price than its flavor."

"See, I told you," bragged Lizzie, raising her hand to give a thumbs-up. Deliberately showing off her tennis bracelet.

"You know who drinks that stuff?" said Pete Hitzer. "That little lush Jasper Beanie. I've picked him up and thrown him in the drunk tank enough times to know his preferences."

"You're right," nodded Jim Purdue. "I've seen Jasper downing Wild Boar on dozens of occasions. He practically lives on it."

"Surely hundreds of people around here drink that same brand," said Cookie, the voice of logic.

"True, but he's the one first comes to mind," attested Pete Hitzer.

"Won't hurt to ask him where he was last night," Chief Purdue said. "Do you think these tracks might match his old junker?"

"Hard to tell," said the deputy. "Snow makes it impossible to identify any tread marks."

"Might be the mailman's car," said Lizzie. Trying to be helpful.

"Too early. Yesterday was a holiday and mail ain't come yet today," explained the deputy. He was showing a lot of promise, what Chief Purdue called a "keeper." Jim planned to retire in the next few years if he could find a suitable successor. Right now it was a toss up between Petie and Evers Gochnauer, the deputy on the night shift.

They walked back up to the house, crowding into Emmy

Buttersworth's warm kitchen. She put on a pot of hot coffee while the two policemen examined the wooden case containing the dueling pistols. Maddy and her ya-ya sisters looked over the men's shoulders.

The case was indeed beautiful, constructed of dark walnut with an inlaid ivory trim. The two flintlock pistols were nestled against a bed of purple fabric, positioned together like inverted Js.

Only Chief Purdue handled the wooden case, keeping fingerprints to a minimum. When they got back to the station they would dust it, looking for any strange prints. Chances are, the deliveryman touched the polished wood.

"Tell me about this feud between your husband and the Bradshaws," the Chief questioned Emmy. She was a pencil-thin woman with short gray hair, the stereotypical look of a librarian or a teacher, though she'd been a farmer's wife for most of her life. Displaying a nervous, skittery nature, it was obvious she would have difficulty carrying on without ol' Sam.

"A bunch of hooey," she replied. "Excuse my language."

"Ma'am?"

"More talk than truth. Sam didn't have no hard feelings over what happened some five generations ago. From what I hear, Sir Samuel Buttersworth deserved what he got. Nobody gets away with selling a crippled horse."

"You're saying there was no bad blood between your husband and Harley Bradshaw?"

"To the contrary. Sam had a fondness for Harley that I never fully understood. They would go fishing together. Harley would sometimes come over for dinner. He liked my watermelon pie, often taking second helpings. He was a polite young man. Sometimes he helped me wash the dishes."

The members of the Quilters Club were exchanging glances. This was contrary to common opinion. Had the feud been nothing more than a local legend that lingered on without basis?

"Well, we've got Harley locked up in our holding cell," sighed Jim Purdue. "Maybe we can get him to talk, tell us why he ran over his friend with the Santa float."

"It's a head-scratcher, to be sure," the woman said as she refilled their coffee cups. "Ain't like Harley. He was close as a son to Sam."

"Thank you for your time, Emmy. You have our condolences for your loss."

"There's got to be an explanation," she shook her head. "As for these ol' guns, you can take them with you. I don't want no part of them."

Family heirlooms indeed!

Chapter Twelve

Another Cold Night in Jail

THAT AFTERNOON Chief Jim Purdue pulled his cruiser up to the gate of Pleasant Glade Cemetery and studied the caretaker's cottage before stepping into the blizzard. He could make out a faint light in the front window. Jasper Beanie was home. His wife would be at work today.

Pulling his cap down over his slick head, the Chief scrambled out of the Crown Vic. Tugging the gate open, he beelined toward the front door, forcing his way through the blowing snow.

Thump-thump-thump he banged on the sagging screen.

"Who's there?" came a hoarse voice.

"Jim Purdue," he shouted. "Open up before I freeze my nose off."

The door cracked enough for an eyeball to peak out. "Whattaya want?"

"To get out of this snow."

The crack widened, the light getting brighter. Without waiting for a formal invitation, the police chief squeezed inside.

"Colder than an ice cube in the arctic out there," he said, shaking the snow off his service jacket. "*Brrrrr.*"

"Wanna drink, Chief? It'll warm you up." Jasper waved his hand toward a bottle of Wild Boar on the table. "I'll get you a clean glass."

"No thanks; can't drink on the job."

"You're on the job?"

"You bet."

"Okay, I surrender. Take me in. I get my usual cell, right?"

~ ~ ~

Harley Bradshaw sat glumly in his cell, watching a re-run of *It's a Wonderful Life* on the flickering 28-inch black-and-white TV outside the bars. He hadn't spoken a word since his lawyer had surrendered him to the police. It was hard not responding to the deputy. He and Pete Hitzer used to hunt quail together. He hated being rude, but his lawyer had been very firm about keeping quiet.

Police Chief Purdue had said they would be transferring him down to Indianapolis in a couple of days. Indy was more equipped to hold longer-term prisoners. With the charge being murder, no way a judge would be granting him bond. He'd have to make the best of it – watching television, reading magazines, playing solitaire, sleeping. He tried to think of it like a paid vacation, courtesy of the State of Indiana. But he would've preferred palm trees and warmer weather. With the storm raging outside, it was cold here in the cell despite the thermostat being turned up high.

Pete Hitzer found him an extra blanket. His Aunt Gloria brought him some Christmas cookies, those star-shaped shards of shortbread glazed with vanilla icing. Mary Bowden, the new dispatcher, provided him with a steaming cup of jailhouse coffee to go with the cookies. And Mark the Shark came by to check on him too. He was definitely on the case. Most lawyers wouldn't even bother coming out in a snowstorm like this.

Harley looked up from the TV as the door to the holding room opened and Chief Purdue ushered in that Beanie guy. This was at the point in *It's a Wonderful Life* when George Baily is slipping Zuzu's petals into his watch pocket. He loved that part. Where George is fibbing to protect someone he loves. As for Beanie, he could tell the little man wasn't inebriated this time. That wasn't good. Him being here was not a good sign.

Harley pretended not to notice as the police chief locked Jasper Beanie into the adjoining cell. Well, there were only two holding cells so where did he expect the second prisoner to go? But it seemed a bit like history repeating itself, time in a loop, the cemetery's caretaker locked up in the next cell again.

Chief Jim Purdue stopped in front of Harley's cell. "I figured out how you did it, just not why," he said.

"Did what?" Harley spoke for the first time.

"When you boys were locked up next to each other yesterday morning, you told Jasper you'd pay him if he retrieved the dueling pistols and delivered them to Emmy."

"You can't prove that," said Harley Bradshaw.

"Maybe not. But I don't have to, since you had the foresight to kill Sam Buttersworth in front of half the town."

~ ~ ~

Beau took the hint when he hadn't had a single customer by lunch. He closed the hardware store for the afternoon and went home. Driving was tricky, his tires slipping and sliding like one of those bumper cars at the carnival. Even though it was only six or seven blocks, he almost wrecked twice.

Beau waved at Jim Purdue as he passed the police

station. The Chief was climbing into his cruiser, probably on his way to get the subpoena to look at Sam Buttersworth's will. Curious that the farmer didn't leave everything to his wife.

Turning on the car radio, Beau found the local news channel. The announcer – a popular radio personality known as Howlin' Horace – warned everybody to stay inside. The storm was coming down off the Great Lakes, swooping its cold winds through Illinois, Indiana, and Ohio. Temperatures were predicted to fall below zero tonight.

No point in thinking about going out to dinner, Beau told himself. Looks like he'd be getting cold turkey sandwiches. Maybe they could find an old movie to watch on the TMC channel. He liked those film noirs like *The Third Man* or *The Big Sleep*.

Maddy and her Quilters Club cronies liked solving mysteries. He preferred watching them on TV.

Chapter Thirteen

The Quilt Arrives

The FedEx truck plowed through the blinding snow, stopping in front of the gray three-story Victorian on Melon Pickers Lane. The driver climbed into the back of the truck to retrieve a bulky package, then ducked his head as he ran through the snow toward the front door. By the time his gloved finger rang the bell, his feet were soaked from the white slush.

"Hello there," said Beau as he opened the door. "You got a package for me?"

"Sure do." The FedEx driver thrust the white box with blue and red designs into Beau's arms. "Sign here."

"Come in and have some eggnog," said Beau as he scribbled his name. "It's cold and wet out here."

"Got a lot of deliveries. This snowstorm is slowing me down. Thanks, though."

"Be careful. This is dangerous driving weather."

"You said it, sir."

As Beau shut the door, he called to his wife: "Maddy, the Christmas quilt's here."

His wife stuck her head out of the kitchen where she'd been baking another batch of cookies. Quite a challenge, but she tried to keep the cookie jar filled this time of year. "Let's take a look at your childhood blankie," she said.

"It's not a blanket. It's a patchwork quilt. Made by Sarah Soldemeir. Didn't you say she's well-known in

75

quilting circles?"

"Known, but not considered top-notch."

Beau held out the FedEx package, hefting its weight. "Heavier than I expected."

"Weight depends on the batting Sarah Soldemeir used. Those old quilts were stuffed with everything from cotton to rags to newspapers."

"This one feels like it's stuffed with rocks."

Beau set the box on the dining room table and pulled at the tab. The cardboard parted with a rasping z-z-z-z-z-z-i-p. He could see a hint of the green holly design with red fabric berries that trimmed the edge of the quilt.

"Spread it out," instructed Maddy. "But handle it carefully. The fabric's old and may tear easily."

Beau took one end; Maddy the other. They stretched the colorful quilt across the length of the table.

"Great balls of fire! That's just as magnificent as I remembered it." The center of the quilt was made up of bright scraps that were stitched together to produce a holiday scene. An old-fashioned feel to the image, Santa was depicted as a portly, white-bearded man, a bag of toys piled on his sleigh.

"That's the Santa from my childhood. But we called him St. Nick."

"That's odd."

"What? That we called him St. Nick? That's short for St. Nicholas."

"No, I mean his costume. It's not the traditional red suit trimmed with white fur. This one's a star-covered coat and stripped pants. More like an Uncle Sam outfit than Santa's."

"See what you mean. But we didn't think anything of it.

It was just St. Nick to us."

"Seems like a strange costume for Santa Claus."

Beau studied the quilt, as if seeing it with new eyes. "I wonder what's the story behind that?"

"We'll have to ask Cookie. She's the historian."

"Here's the invoice Mikey found with the quilt." He held the slip of paper up to the light to read it better. "It says, '*Sold to Minerva Madison One Quilt for the Sum of $20, signed Sarah Soldemeir, April 12, 1852.*'"

"That seems to be proof positive this is a genuine Soldemeir."

"I always thought my mother made it. But it looks like my great-grandmother bought it from this Soldemeir woman. Oh well. It was still a treat to sleep under it on Christmas Eve. Boy, does this bring back the memories."

Ka-thunk!

"What was that?"

"Something fell out of the box." Maddy pointed at an odd-shaped object on the oak floor.

"So it did," said Beau as he picked up the wooden doll. "No wonder the box was so heavy."

"It's a nutcracker. Why would your brother have included that?"

"My mother used to have one exactly like this. A Christmas decoration. Looks like Mikey took it with him when he left home – along with the quilt. Now he's returning them both."

"Your older brother is starting to sound like the Grinch Who Stole Christmas.

~ ~ ~

Darnell Watson was plowing the streets today. His big

green John Deere SP10 tractor was equipped with an oversized snowblade, a perfect machine for scraping the crisscrossed streets of Caruthers Corners. Darnell's sloppy work usually resulted in new potholes in the asphalt. He got paid extra for patching them. A perfect job: paid for creating a problem; paid for fixing it.

He was just turning the corner at Old Farm Road and Second Avenue when he felt a bump. He was always plowing over garbage cans and tricycles and supermarket carts. How could he be expected to see through a thick layer of snow? He didn't have X-ray eyes, for gosh sakes.

He climbed down off the tractor, his padded coveralls making him look like the Michelin Man. Waddling over to the edge of his plow blade, he spotted the object he'd hit.

A metal box.

Chapter Fourteen

Serving the Subpoena

CHIEF PURDUE was on his way over to Dingley & Bratts to present Mark Tidemore with the subpoena requiring him to reveal the contents of Sam Buttersworth's will. No biggie, in that it would have been made public anyway when probated. But this speeded up the process. Time is your enemy in a criminal investigation.

Mark was waiting for him, a copy of the will in hand. He didn't want to stay at the office much longer, given the increasing ferocity of the blizzard outside. Ol' man Dingley had left an hour ago.

"Here you go," he handed off the document. "I'll give you the Cliff Notes: Sam left half his estate to his wife Emmy, the other half to Gloria Bradshaw."

"Gloria –?"

"Don't ask me. I just write them the way the client tells me."

"This sure puts to rest those stories of a feud between the two families."

"Looks that way."

"How big's the estate?"

"Farmhouse, back forty, insurance."

"How much insurance?"

"A million bucks, a new policy."

"A fifty-fifty split, you said?"

Mark nodded. "Yep. Emmy gets the house, Gloria gets

the forty acres. Each gets $500,000 from Global General Life."

"Why Gloria? Why not Harley instead? According to Emmy, her husband seemed to like the boy."

"Like I say, I just write them the way the client tells me."

"Emmy's not going to be pleased to hear about this."

"But Gloria will be, I'd bet."

~ ~ ~

Deputy Evers Gochnauer had just come on duty. His cruiser was parked in front of the DQ on Main Street, him sipping a mocha from a Styrofoam cup, a glazed cruller in his other hand, when someone tapped on his window. It made him jump, sloshing the hot coffee onto his blue pants. He said a word unbecoming of a police officer.

"Roll down your window," said the man whose face was pressed against the glass, distorting his features as if he'd walked into a patio door.

Deputy Gochnauer hit the button, lowering his window. There before him was the countenance of Darnell Watson, the guy with the contract to keep the streets open during a snowstorm. His big John Deere with its compact Plexiglas cab and oversized plow was parked behind the cruiser.

"What the devil, Darnell?" shouted the deputy. "You scared the heck out of me. I spilt my coffee in my lap 'cause of you."

"Didn't mean to sneak up on you, Evers. How could you not see my tractor pull up behind you? It's bigger'n your patrol car."

The deputy frowned and tossed his coffee cup past Darnell Watson, staining the snow brown. "So what d'you want?"

"Found something I need to turn over to you. My plow hit it. A metal box of some kind. Looks important, so I figured I oughta turn it over to the police. That means you, don't it"

"What kind of box?" groused Evers Gochnauer, still irked about the coffee.

Darnell Watson held it up.

The deputy stared at the bank safe deposit box. On the brass surface he could make out the words **Caruthers Corners Savings and Loan No. 7043**.

Chapter Fifteen

Harley's Aunt

GLORIA BRADSHAW had been a looker in her day. At one time she was the most sought-after date for Watermelon Days in the county. Then she went off to school in Muncie; when she returned she refused all invitations, whether to Watermelon Days, church socials, barn dances, or the Rialto movie theater which was still in business back then.

After her brother and his wife died in that electrical storm all those years ago, she took over the role of raising Harley. The couple had been well insured, so Gloria could devote herself fulltime to the task.

Harley grew to be a fine-looking man, square-chinned with a Kirk Douglas dimple. Girls liked him, but he showed little sign of settling down. His job with the USPS kept him pretty busy. He had the mail route on the north side of town.

Chief Purdue pulled up in front of her house around 6:30 that evening. This time of year it was already dark. He'd had his dispatcher call ahead to tell her he was on the way. If Harley wouldn't talk, maybe his aunt would.

She greeted him at the door, looking worse for the wear. The overhead porch light wasn't flattering. Her makeup couldn't hide the puffy circles under her eyes. She'd obviously been crying. Her hair was a bird's nest, barely combed. "How is Harley?" she asked.

"When I left the station half an hour ago, he was eating a big pork cutlet and downing about a gallon of ice tea. The Cozy Café brings food over when we have visitors in our holding cells."

"Visitors," she said the word as if it had a bad taste to it.

"Well, you know what I mean, Gloria." They were on a first name basis. The two had gone to high school together. He'd even taken her out once, before he started dating Bootsie.

"I'm glad to hear Harley's eating well. That boy always did have an appetite."

The Chief chuckled. "Good thing he's gonna be transferred to Indy. Else he'd bust our food budget."

"Transferred?"

"He'll be tried there. We're not equipped to handle long-term incarceration of prisoners being held for major crimes."

"I can't believe he's gone."

"Harley? No, he won't be transferred until tomorrow."

"I meant Sam."

"Yes, that's sure a shame. He'll be missed around here."

"More than you know, Jim."

"I wanted to ask you about the feud between the Bradshaws and Buttersworths –"

She flashed the ghost of a smile. "You don't believe those old stories, do you?"

"What other reason would Harley have had to kill Sam?"

"Well, Jim, that's for you to find out," she said, easing the door closed, leaving him outside in the bitter cold. Interview over.

~ ~ ~

"Deputy Gochnauer's looking for you," the dispatcher's voice squawked over the speaker. The police chief was halfway back to the station. "He says it's important."

"Ah shucks," he muttered. There went any chance of getting home in time for dinner. "Where do I find him?"

"Parked in front of the DQ. He said something 'bout needing another cup of coffee."

"I'm on the way. Call him and tell him to order me a foot long all the way."

Chapter Sixteen

Inside the Box

EDGAR RIDENOUR was watching his favorite program on the Fishing Channel when he got the call. Lizzie was still over at the Madisons, gawking at that ratty old Santa Claus quilt so he pulled on his thick winter coat, walked through the kitchen and into the garage. Once he got the Bimmer's heater going, he hit the button to raise the two-car-wide door and drove into the blinding snowstorm.

He met Jim Purdue and his deputy at the Savings and Loan, used his key to disable the alarm, and ushered them inside. None to soon, his fingers were numb by the time he finished with the key. It must be below zero out there, he told himself.

Caruthers Corners Savings and Loan was a big square stone building with Corinthian columns out front. A large marble-floored lobby with teller stations took up much of the first floor along with the steel-reinforced vault; offices were located upstairs. The Exacq alarm system was state of the art.

The police chief set the brass safe deposit box on a marble-topped table in the lobby. "Can you open it?" he asked the bank president.

Edgar bent to examine the battered box. "Hmm, one of ours alright. How the dickens did it get outside the vault?" He walked over to a computer terminal, fired it up, then entered a password. A few more clicks and he said, "This box belongs to Sam Buttersworth."

"Can you open it?" the Chief repeated.

"You know these take two keys?"

"To remove it from its slot in the vault. I thought you simply lifted the lid after that. But this lid has a lock."

"We have a few high security boxes that require a key to open the lid. This is one of them."

"But can you open it?"

Edgar Ridenour smiled at his best friend. "Do you have a search warrant?"

"No."

"I won't tell if you won't. Let me go get the master key."

~ ~ ~

Inside the safe deposit box, they found three items:

- A copy of the Last Will & Testament that Mark Tidemore, Esq. had drawn up the week before. The subpoena had been unnecessary, it turned out.
- A page that appeared to be torn from an old diary. The handwriting was faint and difficult to read.
- And a Global General Life Insurance Policy in the amount of $1,000,000.

Emmy Buttersworth was the co-beneficiary of the life insurance. Half a mil. An equal amount went to Gloria Bradshaw.

So much for the feud.

Just like Mark the Shark had said, ol' Sam Buttersworth was taking care of both sides. Was this some sort of reparation for an event that happened five generations ago? No, thought the police chief, that couldn't be it. Harley's ancestor killed Sir Samuel, not the other way around. Why should ol' Sam be making amends?

~ ~ ~

That evening the Quilters Club had gathered around Maddy's dining room table to examine the Christmas quilt. "So that's a genuine Soldemeir," said Lizzie, leaning closer to inspect the stitches. "Decent needlework. Stitching's a little loose, but holding up fairly well after a century and a half."

"I didn't know she did holiday themes," said Cookie. "There are a couple of pictures of her creations in *The History of American Quilts*. Mostly nature-inspired designs, as I recall." Nobody ever questioned Cookie's almost-eidetic memory.

"That's a funny suit Santa's wearing," observed Bootsie. She indicated the stars-and-stripes motif. "I didn't know the jolly old elf was so patriotic."

"Didn't the idea for Santa Claus come over from Germany?" said Maddy.

"Sankt Nikolaus and Weihnachtsmann are early German incarnations of a gift-giver who visited nice little children," recited Cookie. "However, he's based on a 4th-Century Greek Bishop named Saint Nicholas. The Dutch version was called Sinterklass, giving us the name Santa Claus."

"St. Nicholas – that's what we called him when I was a boy," said Beau. "Sometimes St. Nick for short."

"That poem 'The Night Before Christmas' by Clement Clark Moore was officially titled 'A Visit from St. Nicholas,'" Cookie reminded them.

"So why would he be dressed up like Uncle Sam?"

mused Lizzie, always concerned with fashion.

"Dunno. This calls for a little research," replied Cookie, stumped for once.

"What's this?" Bootsie picked up the brightly painted nutcracker. "Does it have anything to do with Sarah Soldemeir?"

"Probably not," answered Maddy. "This was just a decoration Beau's Mom used to put up at Christmastime. Beau's brother sent it along with the quilt."

"First thing we should do is get the bill of sale authenticated. Prove that this is really Sarah Soldemeir's handwriting," Cookie said to Beau. "That should establish provenance – from the quiltmaker to your great-grandmother to your mother to your brother to you."

"Dan Sokolowski should be able to help us there," Maddy nodded. Ol' Dan was their go-to guy for anything antiquated.

"What's the point?" asked Beau. "I don't intend to sell the quilt. It's a family heirloom, the quilt my brother and I got to sleep under every Christmas Eve while waiting for St. Nick to come. It brings back pleasant memories of my childhood. One year Santa brought me a red Radio Flyer wagon. My brother Mikey got a Flexible Flyer sled. We used to go down High Jinks on my wagon in the summer, on Mikey's sled in the winter. What a time we had as boys."

"High Jinks?" Bootsie repeated.

"That's what we used to call the hill over behind Jinks Lane. Named after Ferdinand Jinks." Although one of the town founders, Ferdinand Arthur Jinks rarely got mentioned in the history books, squeezed out by the more flamboyant stories about Jacob Ashcroft Caruthers and Col.

Beauregard Hollingsworth Madison.

"That hill's one of the highest points in town," explained Maddy.

"It's no match for Hoosier Hill, the state's highest natural point at 1,257 feet," said Cookie.

"No one would get a nosebleed walking up either of them," laughed Bootsie. Indiana was a fairly flat state.

"Let's concentrate on the quilt," said Cookie. She was fascinated by the design. "The variation in Santa's costume might make it have some historic value."

"Then I'll just set this big green nutcracker up here on the mantle," Maddy said, clearing a space among the Christmas cards. "That'll keep it out of the way."

"Perhaps if this Soldemeir turns out to have any significance Beau will allow me display it at the Historical Society."

"Only if you'll let me borrow it back every Christmas Eve," he joked. "That old quilt was sure good to sleep under on a cold winter night."

Chapter Seventeen

Light Show

*M*ORTIMER HOFSTADTER and his family enjoyed a certain celebrity status in Caruthers Corners. Every Christmas season the Hofstadter's two-story bungalow became emblazoned with about 200,000 twinkling lights – something of a showcase. No other house in the town came close.

Morty claimed you could see his phantasmagorical display from space.

Every year, Ninth Avenue was clogged with bumper-to-bumper automobiles, local sightseers admiring the colorful light show. Chief Purdue usually hired Pappy Geiger, the high school crossing guard, to help direct traffic in front of the Hofstadter house. Geiger liked the holiday overtime, for he had to buy presents for twelve grandchildren. His daughter was more fertile than a fruit fly.

Morty Hofstadter had three kids himself, Billy being the oldest. He'd invited that new girl – Leslie Ann Holmes, the one with the funny accent – over to see the lights. With all the blowing snow there was hardly any traffic on Ninth Avenue tonight. Even Pappy Geiger had gone home, hoping to catch a rerun of *Miracle on 34th Street* on TMC.

Despite the snow, Maddy had dropped Leslie Ann off at the Hofstadter house with the promise to pick her up in two hours after she met with the Quilters Club. Ninth Avenue was too far for Leslie Ann to walk in this weather, but

Maddy's big Ford Explorer managed to push through the snow like a Sherman tank.

"Crikey, that's bright," the girl said as she stood on the sidewalk with Billy to admire the light show. The colored lights pulsed in time to the music as "God Rest Ye Merry Gentlemen" played over a loudspeaker. It made a spectacular backdrop for the Nativity scene on the front lawn.

"We've done this ever' year since I was in First Grade," Billy told her.

"Isn't your brother Timmy in Mrs. Grundy's class this year?"

"Yep. He was one of the elves what got kidnapped by Harley Bradshaw. But after a wild ride, ol' Harley dropped them off at Wal-Mart. I don't think anybody's gonna press charges. An FBI agent told us there wasn't any intent to kidnap, the fourth grade class just happened to be on the float."

"What did Harley Bradshaw have to say when he dropped them off?"

"Timmy said he was complaining about losing some box. It didn't make any sense. My dad says Harley popped his cork, went stark raving mad. Happens sometimes, a blood vessel bursts in the brain or something like that."

"Timmy must have been frightened."

"No, he enjoyed the ride. Wants to do it again."

Ninth Avenue was empty by now, no cars crawling through the snow to see the Hofstadter's Christmas lights. "I'm sorry the weather has kept people away from seeing your house this year," Leslie Ann consoled her classmate. She had to admit she'd never seen such a display in

England. Even the lights at Trafalgar Square and the London Eye didn't compare.

"There's always next year," Billy shrugged, exhibiting a lackadaisical approach to life in a small town.

"True," she said. "But I won't be here. I have to go back to London at the end of the school year."

"But you'll be here for New Year's, right?"

"Yes, I suppose so." She could feel it coming, the invitation to the New Year's Father Time Dance. She held her breath.

"Great. Maybe I'll see you at the dance."

Her world suddenly seemed very dark, despite the gaudy lights before her.

~ ~ ~

After her BFFs left, Maddy drove over to the Hofstadter house to pick up Leslie Ann. To her shock, she met the girl walking home in the snowstorm. Pulling to the curb, she opened the car door and shouted, "Get in!"

"Y-y-yes ma'am," Leslie Ann answered, teeth chattering.

Turning up the heater, she waited for the girl to thaw out. "Are you crazy, out by yourself in this blizzard? What would your parents say if we sent you back to London in a block of ice?"

"T-t-that's funny," Leslie Ann said, trying to hold back the tears. "I f-f-feel like a block of ice."

"Did something happen?"

"No, t-t-that's just it. Nothing happened. Billy didn't invite me to the Father Time Dance."

Maddy hugged the trembling girl. "His loss," she said. "But don't worry, dear. Someone else will ask you."

"I doubt it. There are only f-f-five more days before New Year's. School's out for the holidays and with this bad weather I'm not likely to see any school chums. I'm going to be a wallflower."

~ ~ ~

When they got home Maddy put the girl to bed. As a special treat, she covered her in the Christmas quilt. She was sure Beau wouldn't mind.

Maddy then pulled on her pajamas and slippers before heading down to the kitchen for eggnog. It was nearly midnight.

Surprise, surprise! She caught Beau, head deep in the refrigerator, looking for the spiked version of her eggnog.

"All gone," she said. "My girlfriends drank us dry. Only the tame stuff left."

"Oh well, it has a dollop of Captain Morgan in it," he said resignedly.

"Pooh Bear, because it's you, I'm going to tell you where to find the spare bottle of Captain Morgan. We can add some to the tame eggnog, okay?"

He grinned. "I knew there was a reason I married you."

"For my special eggnog? That's all it took to win your heart?"

"No, that won my liver. The heart took a little more."

"I let Leslie Ann sleep under the Christmas quilt."

He smiled. "That's what it's for."

"Tell me again how your mother came to have that quilt."

"Like I said, I thought she'd made it until we saw that invoice. Now it appears it was handed down from my great-grandmother Minerva Madison. And obviously, she bought it from Sarah Whatzername."

"Soldemeir," Maddy filled in the name.

Beau sighed, as he added a generous helping of Captain Morgan to his glass of eggnog. "I remember my mother used to recite a little poem as she tucked me and Mikey under the covers on Christmas Eve. It was about Santa."

"Do you remember how it went?"

"Word for word."

"Go ahead, then. Let me hear it."

"Okay, it went like this:

"Ho! Santa Claus – our own since Infancy –
"Most tangible of all the gods that be –!
"As first we scampered to thee – now, as then,
"Take us as children to thy heart again."

Maddy smiled, her upper lip covered with foamy eggnog. "I recognize that verse. It's from a poem by James Whitcomb Riley. He's perhaps Indiana's most favorite poet."

"What? My Mom didn't write that poem? My whole childhood was a sham."

Chapter Eighteen

The Box Thief

"GUESS WHO STOLE SAM BUTTERSWORTH'S safe deposit box?" said Lizzie. She was phoning Maddy from the den in the back of the house so her husband wouldn't overhear them talking. This was Quilters Club business. Besides Edgar disapproved of her gossiping.

"Do you mean the one Darnell Watson found on the side of the road?" asked Maddy, looking at the face of her bedside clock. It was 6:30 a.m. She'd hoped to sleep in this morning. Many businesses would still be closed because of the snowstorm.

"Yes, that very one," replied Lizzie. "Number 7043, the box belonging to ol' Sam. Guess who stole it?"

"Beats me." Maddy stifled back a yawn.

"Harley Bradshaw. My husband checked the sign-in records. Harley was the last person to access that box. He must have smuggled it out of the vault under his winter coat."

"How could Harley get access to Sam's safe deposit box? That takes a key and a signature, doesn't it?"

"That's the odd thing," said Lizzie. "He had the key. Sam must have given it to him, no other way he could get one."

"That or he stole it from Sam."

"Not likely. Sam put Harley down as co-owner of the box. He had complete access. All he had to do was sign his name and present a key."

"But why would Harley take the safe deposit box out of the bank. Wouldn't it have been easier to just remove the documents inside it?"

"Edgar thinks Harley may not have had the second key, the one that opens the lid. This was one of those super security boxes that requires two separate keys."

~ ~ ~

Tilly showed up for breakfast, little Agnes in tow. She frequently did this when Mark went into the office early. Without being asked, Leslie Ann took charge of the baby, always a welcome relief for Tilly.

Mark had been tied up day and night. Defending Harley Bradshaw on one count of murder (Sam's) and another count of Grand Theft Auto (if a tractor pulling a Santa Claus float could be defined as an automobile) was the biggest case he'd ever handled. The eleven counts of kidnapping (the abduction of the "elves") had been dropped.

Dingley & Bratts PC wasn't a large firm. Bratts – like Ebenezer Scrooge's Marley – was dead as a doornail. He'd been killed by a falling tree in his front lawn back in '98. A freak accident, they said. That left only Bartholomew Dingley, until Mark joined the firm. Nobody expected that Mark would be there for long. A talented attorney, he was already getting offers from LA and New York. One even from London.

If he handled this high-profile murder case successfully, he could write his own ticket. "Sky's the limit," said Bartholomew Dingley, slapping him on the back. He was very proud of his young protégé.

Publicity about the case had gone viral. The front page

of the *Indianapolis Star-Tribune* announced:

Bradshaw Arraigned in Santa Claus Murder

A little misleading, in that Santa Claus hadn't been murdered. Several people sent condolences to Fatty Johnson's wife. She found that very upsetting.

The *Burpyville Gazette*'s headline was a tad catchier:

Local Man Arrested in Santa's Sleigh Slaying

A radio station in Fort Wayne dubbed it "The Jingle Bells Murder."

TV trucks with dish antennae were parked across the street from the police station. Channel 4 Action News was devoting special coverage to what it called "Santa's Hit-and-Run." Fatty Johnson was threatening to sue. Having been Santa Claus in the Parade, this made it sound like he'd been the killer. That made his wife even more upset.

Two women had already written to Harley, proposing marriage. "I am extremely attracted to a man who takes the Christmas holidays seriously," one letter began. The other was so soaked in Blue Waltz Eau de Parfum that Pete Hitzer could hardly deliver it to the cell without a gas mask.

Mark Tidemore was a workaholic, no doubt about it. Tilly got very lonely sometimes. Thank goodness she had the baby to keep her busy.

"Is Agnes teething yet?" Maddy asked her daughter over a hardy plate of scrambled eggs, thick bacon, buttered toast, and watermelon marmalade. There was no such thing as a continental breakfast in the Madison household.

"Oh, yes. Can't you tell how cranky she is this morning?" Agnes was being fed Gerber's Puree of Bacon, slurping it up as fast as Leslie Ann would shovel it in. The baby smacked her lips, obviously annoyed by her sensitive gums.

"Don't worry, she will be fine," Leslie Ann assured them. "When we finish breakfast I'll recite some nursery rhymes to her. That usually puts her to sleep."

"Nursery rhymes?" said Tilly. "You mean like 'Mary Had a Little Lamb' or 'Star Light, Star Bright'?"

"Mostly English ones, like 'Ladybug, Ladybug' or 'Sing a Song of Sixpence'."

"I'm not sure I know those," replied Tilly.

Leslie Ann paused, spoon in the air. "They are quite common. The 'Ladybug' verse goes like this:

'Ladybird, ladybird, fly away home,
Your house is on fire,
Your children shall burn!'"

Tilly squinched her eyes. "Ooo, that's horrible. Burning children?"

"I'm afraid 'Sing a Song of Sixpence' isn't much better," Maddy patted her daughter's hand.

"Oh?"

Maddy said, "The last verse goes like this:

'The maid was in the garden,
Hanging out the clothes,
When down came a blackbird,
And pecked off her nose.'"

"Mother! Surely you didn't tell those kind of stories to me when I was a child?"

"As I recall your favorite was 'All the Pretty Horses.' That's pretty hideous."

Tilly shook her head, making her blonde hair fly. "I don't remember it at all."

"Let's see if I can remember the lyrics ..."

"I can," volunteered Leslie Ann. "May I recite it?"

"If you insist." Maddy rolled her eyes.

Leslie Ann cleared her throat. "It goes:

'Way down yonder,
In the meadow,
There's a poor little lambie,
The bees and the butterflies,
Pecking out its eyes,
The poor little lambie cried, "Mammy!"'"

"Ugh. I can't believe you recited that to me when I was a child, Mother. It's a wonder I'm not totally warped."

"Mostly I sang you the first verse. It goes:

'Hush-a-bye, don't you cry,
Go to sleepy, little baby!
When you wake
You shall have
All the pretty little horses!'"

"Whew. That's better," sighed Tilly.

"Most nursery rhymes have a dark side," Leslie Ann shrugged. No big deal.

"Perhaps we can stick with 'Mary Had a Little Lamb' for Agnes. "None of that *'pecking out its eyes'* stuff."

Maddy winked at girl. "To please Tilly, maybe you can do 'I'm a Little Teapot' and 'Twinkle, Twinkle, Little Star'?" she suggested.

"Yes, ma'am," said Leslie Ann. Always polite. "But I can tell you Agnes is going to be very disappointed. 'Sing a Song of Sixpence' was her favorite."

Wisely, Maddy decided to change the subject. "How's Mark coming with his big case?" she asked her daughter.

"Gee, I don't know. He never talks about his clients.

Confidentiality and all that. But he doesn't act too worried."

That surprised Maddy. "I'd think it would be a difficult case to win – even for Perry Mason. After all, nearly five hundred people witnessed Harley Bradshaw deliberately run over Sam Buttersworth. Be hard to refute that."

"Mark's good at what he does. Wouldn't surprise me if he proved Harley was in another state at the time of the murder having a cappuccino at Starbucks with the President of the United States and Queen Elizabeth."

The reference to the British Queen made Leslie Ann grin.

~ ~ ~

"So he stole the box," Maddy explained to Beau over breakfast. Tilly had already come and gone. Beau was enjoying a stack of buttermilk pancakes with an egg on top, bacon on the side. On the table there was real maple syrup; none of that Aunt Jemima swill. The 1893 brand name came from a minstrel show ditty, "Old Aunt Jemima," but a former slave named Nancy Green had lent her image to the original packaging. Truth is, Aunt Jemima's Original Syrup contains ten different chemical ingredients to simulate the taste of maple. Mostly it's high fructose corn syrup with caramel coloring.

Maddy chose to forgo the Quaker Oats product on grounds of poor taste, not that it tasted poor. Fact was, her husband preferred Aunt Jemima. But Maddy was determined to save him from himself.

"If Harley stole the safe deposit box, why did he abandon it along side of the road?" asked Beau, puzzled by this new information.

"Beats me," admitted Maddy.

"Likely he didn't abandon it," Leslie Ann interjected politely. She had just finished off her pancakes. Tilly had taken the baby with her, leaving the girl free to enjoy her own breakfast. "After all, the box contained the insurance policy leaving his aunt half the money. He wouldn't want to lose that. Chances are, it fell off the float while he was making his high-speed getaway."

"Fell off the float?"

"Fatty Johnson fell off the float," Leslie Ann pointed out. "So why not the safe deposit box? Billy Hofstadter said his little brother was holding on for dear life."

"Where did Dermot find the box?" Maddy asked.

Beau thought for a moment. "On Second Avenue, out near St. Paul's United Methodist Church. His snowplow turned it up."

"Harley left those school kids off in the Wal-Mart parking lot down near Burpyville," Maddy noted. "Second Avenue would be the route to get him to the Burpyville Road."

~ ~ ~

That morning Fatty Johnson dropped by the hardware store to buy some nails. He was wearing a neck brace, a medical device akin to those cones you put around a dog to keep him from licking a wound.

"Is that from the Parade?" asked Beau as he wrote up Fatty's purchase. When not playing Santa, the white-bearded man worked as a carpenter. Being a steady customer, Beau gave him a 10% discount on all his purchases.

"Yep. I took quite a spill. Bartholomew Dingley is gonna sue the town for me. And I'm filing charges against Harley

Bradshaw for reckless endangerment. I get that money, I might not have to work for a year or two. Wouldn't that be nice?"

"Fatty, I'd think twice before suing Caruthers Corners. The town wasn't responsible for Harley going crazy. All you'll succeed in doing is causing the mayor to raise property taxes to cover the town's legal bills."

"Ain't my problem. I don't own that much land anyhow."

"Fatty, you have a civic responsibility."

"Haw. On top of it all, your son-in-law Mark the Shark oughta be paying me for my services as an expert witness. I could help his case. Sitting up there on the sleigh I could see everything."

"Everything?"

"That's right. I saw Sam Butterworth step directly in front of the float as Harley pulled it out of the Parade. Wasn't Harley's fault. That old fool deliberately stepped in front of a moving vehicle. He kilt himself."

Chapter Nineteen

Here Comes Santa Claus

LATER THAT AFTERNOON Cookie Brown called a meeting of the Quilters Club. She'd left them each a phone message saying: "Assemble!" – that being the code word for an emergency get-together. It had been the call-to-arms for those comic book superheroes, The Avengers.

On cue, the four women gathered at their usual spot, the rec room at the Hoosier State Senior Recreational Center. The big table in the center of the room was cluttered with balls of yarn, rope, ribbons, and string leftover from a work session of the Modern Maturity Macramé Society, a name cribbed from the popular magazine for senior citizens. The macramé folks were a messy lot, often not cleaning up after their textile-making classes.

Lizzie swept the materials off the table with a couple of swoops. As a serious needlecrafter, she had little regard for knot tying and hitching. "There," she said. "Room to spread out."

Prompted by Lizzie's comment, Cookie dumped an armload of books onto the rec-room tabletop. The volumes were quite heavy, her arms tired from carrying them into the building from her car. "I think I've found the answer," she announced.

"What was the question?" asked Bootsie, still unclear why Cookie had called them together on short notice. She had planned to get her hair trimmed this afternoon at the

Helen of Troy Spa & Beauty Salon in Burpyville. She didn't like for her practical pixie-cut to get too shaggy. Besides, Helen of Troy was the place to get good gossip.

"The question is why Santa Claus is wearing striped pants on Beau's Christmas quilt," Maddy reminded her friend.

"Oh right. The Soldemeir quilt," nodded Bootsie. They had been so caught up in the death of Sam Buttersworth, this historical puzzle had been nearly forgotten.

But not by Cookie Brown, Historian Deluxe. "This morning I went down to the big library in Indianapolis to do some research," she said. "I just got back."

"That's a long drive," Maddy said. "If you'd asked, I would've gone with you."

"I thought about calling, but truth is I got an early start. You were probably still getting your beauty sleep," she said, not knowing about Lizzie's early morning calls. She'd been on the road by the time the redhead had got around to phoning her.

"What did you turn up," prompted Lizzie. Hoping for something juicy.

"I knew I'd seen that image somewhere before. And here it is, on the front page of the January 3, 1863, issue of *Harper's Weekly*." She held up the yellowed publication.

"They let you check that out of the library?"

"Not exactly. It's officially on loan to the Caruthers Corners Historical Society."

Maddy squinted to read the fine print. The sprawling illustration was titled "A Christmas Furlough." Drawn by staff artist Thomas Nast, it depicted Santa Claus visiting Union troops, handing out drums and Jack-in-the-boxes as presents.

She studied the picture: There sitting on a gift-laden

sleigh pulled by reindeer was the jolly old elf himself, demonstrating a jumping-jack puppet to a group of soldiers. He was wearing a pointed cap, a coat covered with stars, and a pair of striped trousers – just like the design on Sarah Soldemeir's quilt.

"Thomas Nast?" said Bootsie. "I've heard of him. He's the cartoonist who came up with the donkey and elephant to represent the two political parties."

"Yes," nodded Cookie, her dishwater blonde hair bobbing encouragingly. "He also popularized the depictions we have today of Santa Claus and Uncle Sam."

"That's right," Maddy recalled. "He added the goatee to Uncle Sam and gave Santa his red fur suit."

"This is not a red fur suit," Lizzie pointed to the *Harper's Weekly* cover.

"Nast developed his image of Santa over time," Cookie patiently explained. "Here, look at his 1881 caricature titled 'Merry Old Santa Claus.' White beard, fur-trimmed red suit, rotund belly, smoking a long-stemmed pipe. More like the Santa we know today."

Lizzie stared down at the new image in a book titled *Thomas Nast's Christmas Drawings for the Human Race.* "That's closer," she admitted.

"So you're saying Sarah Soldemeir copied Thomas Nast's 1963 drawing of Santa Claus," Bootsie pieced it all together. "That accounts for the stripped pants."

"Looks like it," Cookie concluded. "Nast kinda confabulated Santa and Uncle Sam, two of his favorite subjects. And ol' Sarah obviously took it from the cover of *Harper's Weekly*."

"Well, that's one mystery solved," said Maddy.

But it wasn't.

Chapter Twenty

A Sleepless Night

SOMETHING KEPT NAGGING at Maddy about the Soldemeir quilt. She slept fitfully that night, still wrestling with the bizarre death of Sam Buttersworth. But snatches of her dreams kept coming back to the quilt.

Getting out of bed, she pulled on her fluffy slippers and padded down the steps to the kitchen for a glass of eggnog. The spiked version, thinking it might help her sleep. She'd made up a batch for Beau. It was 3 o'clock, according to the Westclox of the wall next to the refrigerator.

Something was bothering her about the idea Sarah Soldemeir had copied Thomas Nast's illustration from the 1863 cover of *Harper's Weekly*. Then it hit her: the invoice.

Yes, that was the detail that had been bobbing about in the back of her mind. That invoice had been dated 1852, eleven years before that issue of *Harper's Weekly*.

Time out of joint.

~ ~ ~

That morning Maddy took to her computer. It wasn't hard to find background info about Thomas Nast on Wikipedia. She had barely cracked her 32 volumes of *Encyclopaedia Britannica* since getting the new iMac.

Art historian Albert Boime had written: "As a political cartoonist, Thomas Nast wielded more influence than any other artist of the 19th Century. He not only enthralled a vast audience with boldness and wit, but swayed it time and again to his personal position on the strength of his visual imagination. Both Lincoln and Grant acknowledged his effectiveness in their behalf, and as a crusading civil reformer he helped destroy the corrupt Tweed Ring that swindled New York City of millions of dollars. Indeed, his impact on American public life was formidable enough to profoundly affect the outcome of every presidential election during the period 1864 to 1884."

His best-known work was with *Harper's Weekly*, satirical art that critiqued slavery and crime. Joining the staff in 1862, he worked there for nearly twenty-five years. However, when he left the publication he fell on hard times. In 1902, his old friend Teddy Roosevelt appointed him as US Counsel General for Ecuador. While serving in that country, he contracted yellow fever and died.

Thomas Nast has been called "the Father of the American Cartoon."

She couldn't find any entries linking him to Sarah Soldemeir, other than one line in the woman's biographical profile: "Reputed to be a cousin of noted political cartoonist Thomas Nast."

But that didn't solve the timing problem.

~ ~ ~

Maddy found that sometimes it helped to write specific clues onto 4" x 6" index cards and shuffle them into a sensible order. That often revealed an unseen pattern. So she went to the little oak desk in the anteroom and fetched some cards and a ballpoint pen. The pen was a promotional item handed out by Caruthers Corners Savings and Loan, featuring the bank's name on its plastic shell.

Sitting down at her kitchen table she began to make her

list, moving the cards into proper sequence.

- Sarah Soldemier makes patchwork quilt with "Uncle Sam" Santa.
  - Circa 1852 (based on invoice).
- Cousin Thomas Nast draws "Uncle Sam" Santa for *Harper's Weekly*.
  - 1863 publication date (11 years later).
- Beau's great-grandmother Minerva Madison buys quilt from Sarah Soldemier.
  - 1852 invoice confirms date.
- Minerva Madison hands down quilt to granddaughter Martha Madison.
  - Approx. 1910. A guess.
- Martha Madison uses quilt as Christmas treat for sons.
  - Approx. 1945 – 1960 based on Beau's memory.
- Son Mycroft Madison takes quilt with him when he leaves home.
  - Approx. 1972. An act of spite.
- Mycroft Madison returns quilt to brother Beau.
  - Christmas 2002. An act of contrition?

There you have it, the 1-2-3 sequence of events. Seems clear Sarah Soldemier was the original "designer" of Santa's stars-and-stripe costume eleven years before Thomas Nast drew a similar image. Perhaps he copied her quilt design. What other explanation could there be?

But the patriotic look didn't stick. Nast along with artists like James Montgomery Flagg and Norman Rockwell helped morph it into the red outfit that we accept today.

In the 1920s when Coca-Cola started running those Christmas ads showing a red-suited Santa drinking an icy-cold Coke, the look become an accepted part of America's holiday tradition. An artist named Haddon Sundblom nailed the image in 1931, fixing Santa forever as "a warm, friendly and pleasantly plump man" in a red fur-trimmed suit.

What about that nutcracker? Maddy looked up at the mantle where it sat, on the corner to the right of the miniature Christmas village. The nutcracker was a wooden version of a soldier in a green tunic and tall black helmet, his long jaw designed to crack nuts. A nice Christmas ornament, but unrelated to the quilt.

~ ~ ~

"How do you explain it?" Maddy presented the conundrum to the Quilters Club. They were gathered again in the rec room of the senior center. Fat squares and fabric scraps lay askew on the big table.

All stitching was at a standstill. Maddy had just pointed out the eleven-year gap between Sarah Soldemier's invoice listing *"One Quilt for the Sum of $20"* and Thomas Nast's famous Santa Claus illustration on the cover of *Harper's Weekly*.

"Maybe she saw one of Thomas Nast's earlier drawings in a magazine," suggested Lizzie.

"Nast got his first job with *Frank Leslie's Illustrated Newspaper* in 1856," countered Maddy. Her Wikipedia research had prepared her for this question. "Sarah Soldemeir's invoice was dated four years earlier. He hadn't started working as a professional cartoonist at the time she sewed the quilt. So she couldn't have seen it in a magazine."

"Maybe she saw some of his drawings before he got them published," suggested Bootsie. "After all, Sarah Soldemeir was his cousin. He might've shown her some of his sketchbooks."

"That's a possibility," said Cookie. "I can't think of any other explanation."

"Unless she was exhibiting psychic precognition," said Lizzie. She'd read about stuff like that in the *National Inquirer* and *World Weekly News*.

"What if it were the other way around," Maddy posed the question. She had a great disdain for ESP and "all that malarkey," as she described it.

"What do you mean?"

"What if Nast got his idea for Santa's stars-and-stripes costume from his cousin Sarah's quilt?"

The room was silent for a moment.

Cookie spoke up first. "Then we'd have an amazing historical discovery," she said quietly. "It would be like Dolly Madison stealing the design for the American flag from an old dress pattern."

~ ~ ~

Deputy Evers Gochnauer needed another cup of coffee. The Chief had switched him to the day shift so he could transport Harley Bradshaw to Indianapolis. That boy had barely spoken a word in the past week on the advice of his lawyer. It was going to be a lonely, silent drive to Indy.

Gochnauer had been on the police force for about two years now. This was the first murder case they'd had during that time. Caruthers Corners was a peaceful little town tucked away in the northeastern corner of the state. Being a policeman here was about the boringest job in the world. And that's the way Evers liked it.

He had a favorite place to park his cruiser, under the shade trees behind the E-Z Chair factory. It was an ideal spot to take a nap. If anyone spotted him there in the middle of the night, he had a perfect excuse – it was on his patrol route. But during the day the factory workers ate lunch on the picnic tables under the trees, making it more awkward for him.

That's why he decided to pull his cruiser behind a big billboard on the Highway 21 Bypass. Anybody spotted him there, they would think he was doing a speed trap.

The billboard advertised Kringle Flakes, a new Christmas-themed breakfast cereal. Caruthers Corners was one of six test markets across the United States. The little Midwestern town often got picked for product testing, its demographics representing Middle America. Traditional values, upstanding citizens, that sort of thing.

The cruiser's tires spun as the deputy maneuvered it through the deep snow, positioning it far enough back that it was hard to see from the road. He needed to catch a few undisturbed ZZZZs before making that long haul to Indy with the prisoner this afternoon.

He'd known Harley since the sixth grade. It was going to be awkward, making the run with his old Little League pal wearing manacles. What a dumbass stunt, running over Sam Buttersworth during the annual Christmas Parade. Why not just shoot him in private if you wanted him dead? Why kill him in front of hundreds of witnesses?

Maybe Sam knew his life was in danger. Could that be why he made out his will the week before? Why he took out an insurance policy? Why he bought those guns from Dan Sokolowski – to protect himself?

The puzzler for Evers was why Sam would choose to

march in the Parade with his back to the float Harley Bradshaw was pulling with a tractor. The Straw Hatters could have marched at the end like they usually did, singing an *a cappella* rendition of "Up on the Rooftop." Why flaunt yourself directly in front of your mortal enemy?

Maybe Sam's bad judgment came from being drunk. After all, he'd kind of wobbled off to the side, separating himself from his fellow Straw Hatters just before Harley nailed him. But Dan Sokolowski didn't report that Sam had been drinking when he bought the pistols. And everybody agreed that Sam's fine baritone was as clear and steady as it had ever been, especially when he did a solo turn on "Santa Claus Is Coming to Town" – the Santa Claus float only yards behind him.

This jumble of thoughts was distracting Evers Gochnauer from his nap, but he had his eyes closed and almost missed the speeding Chevy that blew past him on the Highway 21 Bypass. The whine of the Chevy Impala's over-revved engine caused him to look up just in time to recognize Gloria Bradshaw behind the wheel, head bent forward like a determined Gran Prix driver. What the heck was Harley's aunt doing out here in the middle of the day, breaking about six laws including speeding and reckless driving. She was doing 80 if he had to guess. Just up the road he could see the sign that posted the speed limit as 55.

So much for his nap.

The cruiser was still idling to keep the heater going, so he kicked it into gear, flipped on the bubblegum lights on his roof, and gave chase.

Chapter Twenty-One

Page from a Journal

SITTING AT HIS MESSY DESK, Chief Jim Purdue read the tattered page he'd found in the safe deposit box. It appeared to be torn from a diary or a journal. The paper was yellowed with age; the ink had faded to a pale brown, the color of tobacco juice. He had to squint to make out the words.

-127-

"... that Sir Samuel's firearms were olde and riddled with rust. Little surprise that his pistol exploded when he fired it. The flash was somewhat fearsome. The blowback caused the ball to lodge in his forehead. There was no saving he. The garrulous old man had sold a faulty horse, he had picked a fighte with the justly indignant buyer, and his own dueling pistol had betrayed him. In a manner of speaking he died by his own hande. The brother of Sir Samuel presented the guns to Mordecai Bradshaw by way of apology, assuring that no grudge was held between the two families. Thus they swore fealty among themselves to the betterment of ... "

If this document was genuine – and he believed it was

— Mordecai Bradshaw did not kill Sir Samuel Buttersworth in a duel as legend had it. Death came by way of a tragic accident, a faulty flintlock pistol blowing up in the shooter's hand. There could be no hard feelings over Mordecai killing Sir Samuel, because in fact he didn't.

Just as Gloria Bradshaw had said, there was no family feud. And no doubt Emmy Buttersworth was telling the truth about ol' Sam's fondness for Harley.

There went the motive for murder, like smoke dissipating in the air.

Razzlefrazzit! as his friend Beau would say.

~~~

Cookie Brown looked up when the shadow fell across her desk. Truth was, the Historical Society got few visitors. There were no formal exhibits, just boxes of artifacts and a few stray antiques scattered around the room. Over here was a tray of arrowheads; atop the row of filing cabinets were stacks of Blue Willow China; on a chair was a pile of old photo albums. Long rifles and swords decorated the walls. A map of Indiana hung behind the oak desk where Cookie sat.

"Oh! Jim, it's you," she said, surprised to see the police chief standing before her. She'd been so engrossed in a 1913 edition of the *Burpyville Gazette* she hadn't heard him come in. She'd been reading about the Great Flood, one of Indiana's worst disasters. Rainfall topped nine inches in four days, causing runoff, and rising rivers. An estimated 200 had died.

Disasters fascinated her. Some people said she had a morbid outlook. She would argue she was just interested in nature's fury.

"Sorry to startle you, Cookie. I was wondering if the Historical Society might like to have Sir Samuel Buttersworth's dueling pistols? Emmy doesn't want them and they're really not part of the police investigation anymore."

The bespectacled blonde eyed the polished walnut case. "Of course, the Society will take them, not that I know where I'm going to put them. The town needs to build an annex to this building before it bursts at the seams."

He sat the walnut case carefully on her desk. Flipping the latches, he opened the maw of the box to reveal two rusty ball-and-cap pistols on a bed of purple velvet. "One of them's damaged. This journal entry explains how that came to be." He handed her the diary fragment.

"What's this?"

"I found it in Sam's safe deposit box. Looks like a page from an old journal."

She squinted at it, nose close to the paper. "My, this is interesting. Could it possibly be –?" She rushed over to a file cabinet and extracted a cardboard box. Inside was a sheaf of pages, like a book without a cover. "This is what's left of Col. Beauregard Madison historic journal, the one titled *Indian Fighting and Other Activities of Interest by a Colonel in the War of 1812*. A lot of pages are missing. I wonder if this could possibly be one of them?"

Jim Purdue moved around the desk to look over her shoulder. The handwriting seemed to match. Even the ink was faded to the same light brown in both. "You mean this might be a missing page from Col. Madison's journal?"

The document was hand-numbered at the top – 127. She put on a pair of white gloves and flipped carefully through the journal. Sure enough, page 127 was missing.

"Here, let me see," commanded Chief Purdue, comparing the torn edges of the page against the ragged edges in journal. "Bingo!" he exclaimed. "We have a perfect match."

Cookie studied the page, her lips mouthing the words as she read. "Oh my, this changes the historical record. Looks like Martin J. Caruthers got the story wrong."

"I wouldn't trust the word of any relative of Henry Caruthers," the police chief muttered. The mayor wasn't popular, even among his own employees. The Town Council suspected he was embezzling from the Parks & Recreation fund, but no one could prove it.

"I can't wait to share this information with the Quilters Club."

"Bootsie already knows part of it. She's the one who suggested I turn the dueling pistols over to you."

~ ~ ~

Franklin D. Medford, MD, doubled as coroner. His offices were conveniently next door to Yost & Yost Mortuary. That afternoon he phoned Chief Purdue with his autopsy findings.

"Death by blunt force trauma," he stated the official cause of death.

"Could you put it in plain English?" said the lawman. Jim Purdue was a plainspoken man.

"Somebody ran over him with a tractor," said Dr. Medford.

"Don't know why we need to pay you to tell us that. Half the town saw it happen."

"Closer to 20% by my estimation," replied the doctor.

He was known for his dry wit. "Matter of fact, I was standing there in front of the Town Hall myself. But by the time I got to Sam he was a goner."

"A tragic event," said the police chief.

"Not so much as you think."

"What's that supposed to mean?"

"Just what I said. Going fast like that might have been a mercy. Ol' Sam was eaten up inside by cancer. Stage Four. Had another few months at best. Might've been very painful, those last days. Better for him the end came quick, I'd say."

Chapter Twenty-Two

Hired Assassin

THAT AFTERNOON Bootsie and Maddy dropped by the History Society to inspect the newest addition to its collection, the dueling pistols. They were members of the Society's board and technically had to approve any new acquisitions; but in practice they merely rubber stamped Cookie's decisions.

"Where's Lizzie?" the blonde asked, taking off her glasses to rub her eyes. If you looked closely you could believe she used to be a beauty pageant winner. Voted "Most Popular" her senior year at Caruthers Corners High School, no one could figure how she wound up married to roly-poly Bob Brown. A great guy, but not the most impressive catch in school.

"Lizzie's getting her nails done. A lighter red. She may change her hair color to match," Maddy explained their friend's absence.

"I gave her my appointment," said Bootsie. "Decided to let my hair grow out a tad. Don't you think it will look better longer?"

"If you say so," replied Cookie, a woman who paid no attention to style. She'd let herself go, as if having a husband she didn't need to fuss with her looks anymore.

"It will look terrific," Maddy reassured the pudgy brunette.

"I sure hope Lizzie gets home safely," said Cookie. "It

snowing pretty heavily out there."

Bootsie glanced out the window. "We'd all better go soon. Even Maddy's big SUV had trouble getting out here to the south side of town."

"Before we go, show us the guns," Maddy got them back on topic. "That's what we came here to see."

Cookie waved toward the black walnut box, still on her desk. "You'll find the paired dueling pistols in there. They aren't in such great shape, but the case is beautiful. Look at the ivory trim. And examine the way the seams are fitted. I'd guess it came over from England with Sir Samuel Buttersworth. I did a little research. Turns out, he was the Fourth Earl of Dorkshire."

"Does that mean ol' Sam was royalty?"

"Descended from it," smiled Cookie. "You wouldn't have known it to look at a hardscrabble farmer like ol' Sam. That tumbledown old farmhouse off Gruesome Gorge Road is a far cry from a castle."

"Guess we don't have to worry about Emmy. She'll be collecting on that $1,000,000 life insurance policy," commented Bootsie.

"She doesn't get the whole amount," Maddy pointed out. "He left half of it to Gloria Bradshaw."

"That's what I find strange, him leaving so much money to Harley's aunt," said Cookie. "Maybe the families weren't feuding, but that seems excessively generous."

Bootsie shrugged. "Maybe it was intended to be a trust fund for Harley. Emmy said her husband treated him like a son."

"That's a lot of money, even for a real son," Cookie commented. She had no children, so estate planning wasn't high on her list of priorities.

"Maybe it was something else," suggested Bootsie, drawing the words out, teasing, as if she knew something they didn't.

"What else?" demanded Cookie in her non-nonsense manner. "Don't make us guess."

"Jim has a theory," the police chief's wife told them. "What if Sam *hired* Harley to kill him."

"Why would Sam want to die?" asked Cookie.

"Because he was already dying," said Bootsie, going on to tell her about the coroner's findings. "Stage IV cancer."

"Wow! Sam had the Big C," said Cookie. "Who would've known? He looked healthy enough."

"Wait, I've got it!" announced Maddy. The pieces of the puzzle suddenly falling into place. She had that kind of mind. "Sam knew he was dying. Naturally, he would want to provide for his wife. That's why he bought an insurance policy and tied up his affairs with a will."

"But that doesn't work," countered Cookie. "The insurance company wouldn't pay off on death from a preexisting condition."

"Exactly," continued Maddy, now on a roll. "Sam's estate could only collect if he died of some other cause. Like getting run over. And so there would be no question about the cause of death, he arranged to get himself run over in public. By a tractor driven by his friend Harley in the Christmas Parade."

"And – *voila!* – his wife's future financial needs are taken care of," Cookie finished the thought.

"There it is, the motive for murder," said Maddy, proud of herself. "Insurance fraud."

Bootsie nodded. "Maybe that's why half of the estate goes to Harley's aunt, an indirect payoff to him for acting as assassin. Harley couldn't get the insurance money himself, because murderers aren't allowed to profit from their actions. But paying it out to a family member might be a workaround."

Maddy summed it up. "Harley killed Sam Buttersworth alright. He was paid to do it as part of an insurance scam."

The Quilters Club had solved its case. At least they thought so at the time.

Chapter Twenty-Three

The Sleepover

GLORIA BRADSHAW SAT in the police chief's private office. Deputy Gochnauer had brought her in on charges of speeding and reckless endangerment. He sat to one side of her, looking like a fisherman showing off his catch.

The older woman looked worse for the wear, a white bandage wrapped around her head like a scarf. One eye would be turning black. She'd taken the curve at Old Farm Road at close to 80 MPH, her car spinning off the snow-covered highway and ending up in the middle of Ben Bentley's soybean field. Lucky it didn't flip. But she took a few bumps before the Chevy came to a stop in a snowdrift.

"What was the big hurry?" Chief Purdue asked, perched on the edge of his desk like a principal scolding an errant student.

"I heard Harley was going to be transferred to Indianapolis today. I was afraid I'd miss seeing him before he left."

"Evans here is going to escort him. But he can't do that while chasing your Chevy Impala on snowy roads. It's a wonder you didn't get both him and you killed."

"Save the lecture, Jim. Just give me my speeding ticket and let me see Harley before your bulldog here drags him off to Indy."

"Bulldog –?" growled the deputy, for a moment looking exactly like the canine in question.

"Everybody calm down," said Chief Purdue. "What's so important for you to tell Harley that you'd risk your life getting here in this weather?"

Gloria Bradshaw hesitated. "I just wanted to wish him well. He's never been away from home for any extended period of time."

"He may be looking at thirty years to life in this case," snapped Deputy Gochnauer, still fuming over the 'bulldog' remark. "I'd call that 'extended.'"

She was close to bursting into tears. "B-but there were extenuating circumstances –" she sputtered.

Chief Purdue stood, looming over her like a storm cloud. Deliberately trying to be intimidating. "What extenuating circumstances? It's about time you or Harley speak up. Mark Tidemore's not gonna be able to save his skin if he doesn't get any help."

"Mark knows the score. He'll make the case in court."

"Look, I know you raised Harley," said the police chief. "But he's got to stand on his own two feet for this one."

"There's more to this than you know," she retorted.

"Do you think I'm just a dumb cop, Gloria? I know Sam hired Harley to kill him. Because of the insurance."

"Nobody hired Harley," she hissed. "This was an act of mercy – euthanasia."

"What about the money he's getting through you? I've seen Sam's will."

"That money's not for him. Sam wanted me to have it."

"Why would Sam give you such a big wad of cash?"

"I'm not saying another word without Mark Tidemore present. And neither will Harley."

~ ~ ~

Lizzie Ridenour loved gossip; in fact, she thrived on it like a potted plant sucking up water. And a trip to the beauty salon was the place to find it. Helen of Troy was, to quote Maddy, "Gossip Central."

Today, while doing her hair, Margie Yost happened to mention that there might be some holes in Gloria Bradshaw's history. "Them Bradshaws act like they're high and mighty," yammered Margie as she dyed Lizzie's hair, the chair tilted back to let her head rest in the pink porcelain sink. "But that Gloria's a big phony."

Lizzie listened, showing great restraint in not questioning Margie's story. After all, she knew Harley had dumped the owner of Helen of Troy after a few dates. Kirk Douglas chin or not, he obviously didn't want to be tied down.

"Gloria claims she studied at Ball State, but my Uncle Floyd went there the same year Gloria says she was there. Sure, it's a big school, but hometown kids stick together. My uncle was from Caruthers Corners, y' know. He swears she never set foot on that campus in Muncie. Now why would she lie about something like that, else she was putting on airs. I bet she never even went to college. Probably took the year off and went up to Chi-Town with her brother and his preggers wife."

"Are you sure about this?" asked Lizzie, eyes squinted to avoid the red dye. It contained peroxide to lighten the shade of her hair.

"Uncle Floyd's got no reason to not tell the truth about a thing like that. He knew Gloria Bradshaw. Heck, he was one of her many suitors. If she'd been on that campus, he'd have sniffed her out like a hound after a bitch in heat."

131

"Hurry it up," urged Lizzie. "I've got to get home before the snow gets worse." What she really meant was she couldn't wait to share this juicy tidbit with the Quilters Club.

~ ~ ~

The snow was coming down like a white curtain, visibility limited to about ten feet. No way Deputy Gochnauer was going to transport the prisoner to Indianapolis today. Chief Purdue wasn't even sure any of them could get home in this weather. Turns out, he was right.

"Governor just declared this part of the State a disaster area," his dispatcher reported. She kept a small TV tuned to Channel 4 Action News on a corner of her desk.

"Snow looks pretty deep out there," concurred Jim Purdue, looking out the station's front window. "I doubt even a car with chains could get up Main Street right now."

"That weather girl on Channel 4 says this might be worse than the Great Blizzard of '78."

"Yeah, that was a bad one," agreed Evers Gochnauer.

Known as the White Hurricane, that historic winter storm had raged from January 25 through January 27, 1978. Its barometric pressure was the third lowest non-tropical atmospheric pressure ever recorded in the mainland United States ... and lowest ever in the Midwest. By the second day Indianapolis International Airport had to be closed because of whiteout conditions. Temperatures dropped to zero. Wind chills remained at a bone-chilling 40 to 50 below zero nearly all day. More than 15 inches of snow fell in Indianapolis; a whopping 36 inches hit South Bend.

"Looks like we're gonna have us a sleepover," the police

chief said. "Nobody's going home in this snowstorm."

There was general mumbling, frowns of resignation.

Jim Purdue thought about the logistics: He would let Gloria Bradshaw bunk down in the cell next to her nephew. He had cut Jasper Beanie loose earlier today, so it was empty. He could sleep in his office chair. Gochnauer and the dispatcher would take the couches in the outer office. He'd already phoned Petie Hitzer telling him not to try to come in.

Crimefighting would have to take a hiatus tonight.

~ ~ ~

Bootsie was used to her husband's long hours. However, she wasn't happy to hear that he was stranded at the station in the middle of a snowstorm. Too bad he couldn't get home for dinner. She'd made a pot of chili, the kind he liked. Beans, cheese on top, chopped onions. Lots of meat. More than enough to feed him and his entire force, if it came down to it. Prisoners too.

"Maybe I could bring you some chili if the snow lets up."

"Don't even think it," Jim warned. "This is going to be a bad night."

"But —"

"No buts. Even the Cozy Café can't get a delivery to us ... and they're just two doors down the street."

Looking out her kitchen window, Bootsie knew he was right. She couldn't even see the light from the lamppost in the front yard. No way she could get to Main Street. Jim's police cruise had snow tires with chains, but the Goodyears on her Toyota Rav-4 were getting slick. She'd been meaning to buy a new set, but the Christmas season had gotten in the way.

"Stay warm," his wife said as they hung up.

She continued stirring the pot of chili, letting her thoughts drift. She couldn't help thinking about Sam Buttersworth's insurance scam. Now that it was known, would Global General Life refuse to pay off, leaving Emmy destitute?

Sometimes uncovering the truth had unintended consequences.

Just then Bootsie's phone rang. Hoping it was Jim telling her he'd found a way home, she picked up the receiver and said, "Hi, honey."

"Are you that happy to hear from me?" laughed Maddy.

"Oh, I thought it was Jim."

"Beau says everybody is stranded. He's still at the hardware store. Lucky he had that new heating system put in last year. Thermometer says it's ten below outside."

"I hope Lizzie got back from Burpyville. Margie Yost is not the fastest scissors on the tray when it comes to hairstyling."

Maddy chuckled at the truth in that statement. Margie was good but slow. "Don't worry, Edgar called to say Lizzie's safe at home. He sent someone from the bank to drive her back. But Cookie's stuck out at the Historical Society. I talked with her just a few minutes ago. Looks like she'll have to spend the night there."

"That building doesn't have a proper heating system. Just a cast-iron stove."

"There's plenty of coal in the basement. She'll keep warm."

"What about food?" asked Bootsie, thinking of the pot of chili simmering on her electric stovetop.

"You know she keeps candy bars in one of her file cabinets. Our girl won't starve."

"That's right. She has a sweet tooth for Snickers and Milky Ways. Don't know how she avoids cavities."

"Cookie's very fussy. She brushes after every meal."

"And you're safe at home?"

"Right here in my toasty kitchen on Melon Pickers Lane."

"This is the worst weather we've had in years," sighed Bootsie. "I was watching the weather channel. It said the governor has declared northeastern Indiana a disaster area."

"Sign me up for a week in the Bahamas. But I was calling for another reason. I have some big news."

"Not because you were worried about me, home alone in the middle of a blizzard?" sighed Bootsie.

"Remember, I'm home alone too. You get no sympathy from me, dear."

"Drat. So what's your big news?"

"Actually, it's Cookie's big news. Trapped at the Historical Society, she decided to clean up those dueling pistols your husband dropped off today. She was removing them from the walnut case when the damaged pistol snagged onto the velvet, pulling up a corner of the cloth and revealing a stash of letters underneath."

"Letters?"

"Love letters, actually."

"You mean letters between Sir Samuel and his wife – what was her name? – Mary?"

"No, between Sam Buttersworth and Gloria Bradshaw."

"What? That can't be right. Sam's been married to

Emmy for forty years. They were going to renew their vows, remember?" The police chief's wife had a moralistic streak. Husbands didn't stray in Caruthers Corners. The biggest scandal going was Jasper Beanie's wife and the mayor.

"Guess that's why the letters were hidden away."

Bootsie said, "One thing's for certain: That gives a whole 'nother view of why ol' Sam included Gloria in his will."

Chapter Twenty-Four

Hero of the Night

DARNELL WATSON turned out to be the hero of the night. Tucked inside the warm cab of his John Deere tractor, Darnell plowed his way out to the Historic Society to rescue the stranded secretary.

However, instead of taking Cookie to the farmhouse she shared with her husband, he pushed his way straight down the center of Main Street to deliver her at the square block building that housed the Caruthers Corners Police Station. Chief Purdue was waiting at the door when the man in the padded coveralls ushered his passenger down from the oversized tractor.

"Hurry up, Darnell. Get her inside," shouted the police chief. He could see that Cookie Brown was shaking like an out-of-balance washing machine inside her thin winter coat.

Bootsie had phoned her husband to tell him of Cookie's discovery, the stack of love letters hidden inside the dueling pistols' case. He'd immediately called Darnell, dispatching him to the little clapboard building on the south side of town that housed the Historical Society.

At first Darnell had grumbled, for he was already home, his snowplow parked for the night in the big pole barn out back. He was enjoying a beer and had just popped a Digiorno frozen pizza in the oven. No way he wanted to face that bitter cold again. Despite the triple layer of wool socks, his toes were still numb from being out there earlier today.

However, Darnell's willingness to help came to the surface when Chief Purdue reminded him that his contract for snowplowing and pothole repair would be coming up for renewal with the Town Council next month. Suddenly, he was Mr. Helpful.

Although visibility was limited, Darnell Watson knew the maze of streets like a map inside his head. Within an hour he arrived at the police station with his shivering passenger, even having stopped by Cozy Café to pick up a take-out order for a dozen hamburgers with fries.

~ ~ ~

At Chief Purdue's request, Cookie Brown had brought the packet of love letters directly to the police station. Darnell Watson had about the only vehicle capable of getting through this snow. Must be ten inches on the road by now.

A pink ribbon held the stack of letters together. Cookie had retied it after perusing these missives of the heart. Being a historian, she didn't feel like it was snooping to read them. By her reasoning, these documents revealed the past – making them historical artifacts no different than the 1856 Declaration of Incorporation of Caruthers Corners or Col. Beauregard Hollingsworth Madison's famous *Indian Fighting* diary.

"Here you are," she presented the letters to the police chief as if serving him a slice of birthday cake. "Some of these are pretty steamy," she warned, glancing reproachfully at Gloria Bradshaw who was sitting in a chair next to Jim's desk.

"Thanks, Cookie."

"Thanks for rescuing me."

"No problem, although being cooped us with us here at the police station may not seem much like a rescue by time the night's over."

"Hey," protested Darnell Watson, drinking a cup of steaming-hot jailhouse coffee, "I'm the one what picked you up. Best you thank me. I sure as heck didn't wanna go out in that snowstorm tonight. This is worse'n the Great Blizzard of '78."

Gloria Bradshaw pointed at the letters in Cookie's hands, recognizing the bundle by the pink ribbon. "That's private correspondence. You can't read those."

"'Fraid we can," said the police chief. "They were found in property donated to the Historical Society."

"It's a federal crime to read someone else's mail," Gloria insisted. "Go ask Harley —" she nodded toward the jail cells in back "— he's a mailman. A government employee. He'll tell you it's against the law."

"Not when the mail has been discarded. These were found in the bottom of a gun case given to the Historic Society by its rightful owner, Mrs. Emmy Buttersworth."

"Wasn't hers to give."

"Matter of fact, it was. Her husband purchased the gun case from Dan's Den of Antiquity on the very day he died."

"But he was buying it back for me, not her. When I learned Harley had sold that box of guns to Daniel Sokolowski, I phoned Sam and asked him to get it back. Harley didn't know that's where I hid my letters from Sam. Nobody did, till that nosy busybody found them." She gave Cookie the Evil Eye.

"Hey, I'm not the one who had an affair with a married

man," sniffed Cookie. The Methodist upbringing coming out.

"Yeah? You weren't so perfect in high school, Miss Beauty Queen." A little jealousy coming out. "I could tell tales."

"You two calm down now," ordered Deputy Gochnauer. "This is a police station – not *The Jerry Springer Show*."

Police Chief Purdue waved the letters at Gloria, "So you had a fling with Sam Buttersworth. What else aren't you telling us?"

"It wasn't a fling. It was a genuine love affair. But he couldn't leave Emmy. He was a loyal husband."

"Not loyal enough," muttered Cookie, unkindly.

Gloria Bradshaw shot her a death-ray look. "That was over thirty years ago. What does it matter now?"

"Mattered enough that your nephew's sitting back there in a jail cell," said the police chief.

Chapter Twenty-Five

A Packet of Love Letters

MADDY MADISON phoned her daughter to make sure things were okay at the Tidemore household. A few days ago Mark had said they were having trouble with their ancient oil furnace. However, Tilly reported that she and the baby were comfy-cozy. Meanwhile, Mark was stuck at the office with the legal secretary, 80-year-old Doris Grossman.

Maddy reported that Tilly's brothers had phoned to check on them. The record snowstorm was all over the news. Northeastern Indiana was faring even worse than Chicago.

"What did you find out about that old quilt Uncle Mikey sent Dad?" Tilly wanted to know.

"Not much. Just that it's a genuine Soldemeir. Not very good workmanship, but it might have some historic value because of its design."

"Historic? I thought it was just a patchwork depiction of Santa Claus ...."

"That it is. But apparently it's the earliest known depiction of St. Nick in a patriotic costume."

"Patriotic? I've never seen Santa wearing anything other than a red suit."

"Back in 1863 *Harper's Weekly* published an illustration of Santa wearing a stars-and-stripes outfit. That's the only other instance I'm familiar with. So it makes

Beau's quilt quite rare."

"Sounds like it belongs in a museum."

"Actually Beau is thinking of giving it to you. To continue the family tradition with baby Agnes. His mom used to let the boys sleep under it on Christmas Eve. It was considered a childhood treat."

"I'd guess that old quilt has a lot of sentimental value to Dad."

"Yes, it does. One of his few connections to his brother Mycroft."

"Why did Uncle Mikey leave home and never contact the family again – till now."

"I may as well tell you. Your Uncle Mikey is gay. He had a big fight with his parents when he came out. They didn't approve. Midwestern values and all that. And it *was* thirty years ago. So he went to New York City and worked in the theater. Had a good life on his own, apparently. He was once nominated for a Tony."

"Gay? But I thought Dad said Uncle Mikey had a son."

"Two sons, actually. He tried the straight life for a while, got married, had some kids – your cousins Matthew and Mycroft Jr. – but it didn't work out. He's who he is, no amount of social pressure could change that."

"So I have a gay uncle?"

"You have a very talented uncle. If I've taught you anything, it's to accept people for who they are."

"Oh, I'm not being judgmental, Mom. I think it's cool to have a gay uncle. None of my friends at the Garden Club can make that claim."

"Don't be so sure about that. There are more gay people in Caruthers Corners than you might think."

"I don't know of any, other than Mr. Micherson and his partner." Oliver Micherson owned a flower shop on the far side of town. His longtime companion was Jeff Brown, younger brother of Cookie's husband.

"People like their privacy," Maddy pointed out. "As long as there's a social stigma, many gays will keep their personal lives to themselves. Especially here in Indiana. Over all, the state's pretty conservative."

"I hope I get to meet Uncle Mikey some day. He's been a missing limb on the family tree far too long."

Chapter Twenty-Six

A Hard Night

BEAU SLEPT OVER at the hardware store. No, not on a bed of nails. He made himself a comfy pallet atop some bags of potting soil. It was like renewing his connection with the earth, like when he and his brother Mycroft slept in their pup tent in the backyard.

Having brought it to work with him, he curled up under the Christmas quilt. It kept him warm, just like on all those Christmas Pasts. Before the snow got so bad, he'd had a chance to show the quilt to Dan Sokolowski, whose antique shop was located only a few doors down.

Sokolowski had authenticated it as a genuine Sarah Soldemeir. He'd found a book showing one of her creations with a similar design, an autumn quilt with maple leaves that was stylistically reminiscent of the holly edging around the Christmas quilt. The antiques dealer had offered to buy the quilt for $1,000, but Beau turned him down. He wanted to keep it in the family, an heirloom of sorts.

Beau brewed himself a cup of coffee and ate a stale donut left over from yesterday's visit to the Dairy Queen. He usually bought crullers and bear claws to share with his customers.

Maddy phoned her husband around 9 a.m. The snow was still swirling outside, but nowhere nearly as bad as last night's storm. Cars parked on the street were only identifiable as white mounds. Nobody could be seen on the sidewalks. Tree limbs were overburdened with snow, some to the breaking point.

"Sleep well?" she asked.

"Like a rock. In fact that's what it felt like I was sleeping on – rocks."

"I missed having my Pooh Bear to cuddle with last night," she replied.

"If it's calmer outside, I'm going to come home. I could use a hot shower and a good breakfast. That leftover donut didn't do the trick."

"Bacon and eggs coming up," she promised. "But be careful. The radio says roads are still impassable in places."

"I'll bring the quilt home. Dan says it's the real deal, just like you gals suspected. I always thought my mother made it. But guess I had it wrong."

"What puzzles me is how your great-grandmother came to acquire the quilt. She lived here in Caruthers Corners all her life, never traveled. Sarah Soldemeir lived in one of the Burroughs of New York City, according to her biography."

"Where did you find a biography about her? She's pretty obscure, according to Dan Sokolowski."

"Online. You can find anything online. All you've got to do is Google it."

"Google? Like in Barney Google – that old comic strip character?"

"More like his 'goo-goo-googly eyes.' Google is the name of an Internet search engine." Maddy was becoming quite the computer whiz since Beau bought her that iMac last summer. "Helps you find stuff."

"Engine? I thought your computer ran on batteries." Beau remained a complete Luddite. Even the cash register at the hardware store was the antiquated mechanical kind, where little pop-up flags showed the prices he rang up. *National Cash Register Company 1884* was emblazoned on the brass façade. Dan Sokolowski had tried to buy it too, saying the register was a collector's item.

"What else did Daniel tell you about your quilt?"

"Just that the stitching was a little loose."

"I could have told you that. The biography said she was known for loose stitches."

"What else did that bio tell you about Sarah Soldemeir?"

"*Born circa 1820; died of yellow fever in 1877. An American needlecrafter. Third cousin of noted artist and political cartoonist Thomas Nast. About ten years ago there was a showing of her quilts at the American Handicraft Museum in Brooklyn.* Nothing really new."

"Anything to report on Sam Buttersworth's death?"

"A biggie. Cookie turned up some *billet doux* between Sam and Gloria Bradshaw."

"*Billet* ... what?" Beau didn't speak French, although he'd mastered a few salty phrases from when he was a dog soldier in Vietnam. France had ruled that country as a colony until its defeat in the Indochina War back in 1954. Beau had been there in the '60s.

"Love letters," his wife translated. "Seems Gloria and Sam used to be a hot item. But all hush hush. Nobody suspected until now. These letters were stuffed in the bottom of that case holding the dueling pistols."

"Now ain't that a kick in the pants," Beauregard Madison mused. "Ol' Sam getting it on with Harley's aunt. And everyone thinking there was acrimony between the two families. People can fool you."

Chapter Twenty-Seven

Sunday Morning Coming Down

WITH THE SNOW letting up, Mark Tidemore managed to make it down to the police station. Darnell Watson had gone out early, clearing the entire length of Main Street from Town Hall to Family Dollar Store. The sporadic traffic left slushy tracks on the dark asphalt. A few hardy townspeople could be seen on the sidewalks, heads down, walking against the wind. Snow still eddied in the air, what Mark's mother used to call "Polar Bear Weather."

Church bells were ringing in the background, reminding folks that it was Sunday morning. No casualties – everyone had survived what they were calling the Great Snowstorm of '02. Many were heading to Pleasant Meadows Church or First Baptist or St. Paul's United Methodist to thank Jesus.

Within fifteen minutes, the young lawyer had secured Gloria Bradshaw's release. Chief Purdue agreed to drop the speeding and reckless driving charges. And since there was no law against swapping love letters with a married man, she was free to go.

Harley still wasn't talking, other than to his aunt and his lawyer. He and Mark Tidemore huddled in a far corner of the cell, their voices sounding like the hum of electricity.

Given the murder charge, there was no chance of Harley getting released on bond. The lawyer merely said, "See you in court," as he bade goodbye to Chief Purdue.

Simply a statement of fact. After all, Jim Purdue was his wife's godfather, practically a member of the family. This was just business, what lawyers did. Everyone deserved a fair trial, even if several hundred upstanding citizens saw you do it.

But eyewitnesses are known to be unreliable. Mark Tidemore was basing Harley's defense on the coroner's report and a Super 8 film shot by Oliver K. Micherson, owner of Personally Yours Flowers & Gifts.

~ ~ ~

Ollie Micherson had been standing on the steps in front of the Town Hall, a position that gave him a clear view of the Christmas Parade. He was filming the festivities with his Argus Model 801 Super 8, a relic from the '70s. The film stock was hard to find these days, but he knew a company in Amarillo, Texas, that could supply the cartridges and develop them too. He had an old Bell & Howell projector. None of that newfangled digital equipment for him. He had filmed ten years of vacations to P-Town on Super 8 reels, so why change now?

His niece was one of Santa's elves on the reindeer float. She was in the fourth grade this year. She got to sit in the sleigh with Fatty Johnson, waving at her Uncle Ollie as the float drifted past Town Hall.

Ollie Micherson panned his camera to catch Suzie as she smiled in his direction. The angle caught the back of the float, the tractor between the plastic reindeer, the Straw Hatters marching in front, and a big red Caddy with Mayor Caruthers sitting high in the backseat.

Micherson wouldn't notice it until he played back the film, but the Straw Hatter on the left took a sidestep away from the other three singers, as if deliberately distancing himself.

All of a sudden the tractor pulling Santa's sleigh lurched forward, picking up speed as it swerved directly at the Straw Hatter on the left. The impact made a loud *thunk!* And then the float bounced over the body. *Ka-thunk-thunk!* Making a sharp left turn at the next corner, the float bounced Santa right out of his seat on the sleigh, leaving the jolly old elf sputtering and cursing as he lay sprawled in a snow bank. Without a "Merry Christmas to all and to all a good night" Harley Bradshaw sped away with Miss Grundy's fourth graders in tow.

And Oliver K. Micherson had it all on film. He felt like Abraham Zapruder.

Chapter Twenty-Eight

Sam's Suicide

TILLY PHONED Dingley & Bratts to check on Mark, but the legal secretary said he had already left, heading down to the police department to secure the release of a client. She was still at the office, waiting for her husband to come pick her up. She was afraid to drive in all this snow.

"Mark's going to get Harley Bradshaw released?"

"No, dear. He's there for Harley's sister. She got arrested for speeding yesterday. He'll likely get her off with a fine."

"What about Harley?"

"Oh, that boy will have to wait for his day in court," clucked Doris Grossman. She had a hoarse smoker's voice, the result of a 60-year habit. "But don't worry, your husband's got a good defense planned for him. He'll probably get off with a few years in the State Prison. Involuntary manslaughter, leaving the scene of an accident, a few minor charges."

"That would take a miracle," Tilly declared. "Half the town saw him do it."

"Only 487 known witnesses. Mr. Tidemore did a survey. Hired a telemarketing company to call everybody in town and ask if they saw the suicide."

"Suicide?"

"That's right. Mr. Tidemore has located a home movie someone shot of the parade that clearly shows Sam

Buttersworth stepping in front of the float. Now that we know Sam had cancer, it's obvious his death was a deliberate suicide."

~ ~ ~

"Mark the Shark's claiming it was suicide," Maddy shared the information. She'd just got off the phone with Tilly. "He supposedly has a film showing that Sam deliberately stepped in front of the float."

Bootsie shook her head. "He might convince a jury, but not me. There was more going on than that. Harley speeded up."

"It's a dead end," Cookie sighed. "Harley refuses to talk. So does his aunt."

"Anybody they might have confided in?" asked Maddy.

"Margie Yost says Gloria has no close friends, nobody she would confide in," offered Lizzie, this info from her recent visit to Gossip Central.

"What about her nephew?" said Cookie. "Does he have anyone he'd talk with?"

"Didn't have a girlfriend. Apparently hung out with Sam. Worked as a mailman, delivering mail all day, alone in his car," Lizzie ticked off the list.

"Sounds pretty much like a loner," Bootsie acknowledged. "And since Sam's death, he's been locked up in jail, talking to no one but his lawyer and his aunt."

"Well, you can be sure Mark's not going to share any info," Maddy said. "He doesn't even tell his wife about his clients."

"And Gloria clammed up when Jim tried to question her," Bootsie added.

"There is someone else Harley Bradshaw talked with,"

Leslie Ann meekly spoke up. As a junior member of the Quilters Club, she didn't want to overstep her bounds.

The four women looked at the girl and said as one: "Who?"

"That man who works at the cemetery. He was in the adjacent cell. He admitted Mr. Bradshaw paid him to return the dueling pistols to Mrs. Buttersworth. So they must have talked."

Chapter Twenty-Nine

Jasper's Visitors

JASPER BEANIE was surprised to find the four women standing on his doorstep. He'd had more callers this past week than in all the years he'd been cemetery caretaker combined – first Chief Purdue, then a group of Jehovah's Witnesses, a woman trying to find her husband's grave, some lost Boy Scouts, an itinerant Bible salesman, and now these fine ladies.

"Nancy Ann," he called over his shoulder. "We got more company."

When the visitors shuffled into his tumbledown cottage, Jasper noted the girl behind them. She must be the Hands Across the Sea student staying with the Madisons. He'd heard she was from London. That was the place where the bridge was falling down. Maybe she would be safer over here.

"Can I offer you ladies a drink?" the smarmy little man waved toward a half-empty bottle of Wild Boar on the table. "Got whisky or Old Milwaukee or water – takes your choice. Might find a Pepsi for the young lady here."

"Nothing, thanks," replied Maddy, speaking for the group "We just wanted to ask you a few questions about Harley Bradshaw."

"Harley Bradshaw?" repeated Nancy Ann Beanie, striding into the disheveled living room. Housekeeping was obviously not her strong suit. "Why should Jasper know anything about that cold-blooded murderer?"

"He shared the cell next to Harley twice this week," answered the police chief's wife. "We thought they might've had a chance to chat."

"Jasper, did you talk with that terrible man?" Nancy Ann eyed her husband like a bird inspecting a bug.

"Just to pass the time, dear. Harley weren't allowed to talk to the police, his lawyer's orders."

"We know Harley paid you to leave those dueling pistols on Mrs. Buttersworth's doorstep," interjected Cookie. The Historical Society had been the ultimate beneficiary, so she decided to start there.

"He didn't pay me that much – just $10. Said he'd give me the money when he got out."

"You may be waiting quite a while for that money," Lizzie muttered under her breath. "Twenty or thirty years would be my guess."

"Jasper, you're going to get arrested for a stunt like that," his wife reprimanded. As the mayor's assistant, she had her dignity to maintain.

"Already did. That's why I was in jail the second time."

His wife scowled. "I thought that was for another bender." The police no longer bothered to arrest Jasper Beanie for drunk and disorderly; they just provided a jail cell for him to sleep it off – his "second home."

"No, Chief Purdue picked me up here at the cemetery. I didn't even get to have a drink before he hauled me in. I hate going in dry like that."

"Did Harley tell you why he did it?" asked Maddy.

"Did what?"

"Why he ran over Sam Buttersworth," Lizzie snapped, unable to hold back her frustration.

Jasper Beanie looked from Lizzie to the girl beside her – both redheads. "Is that your daughter?" he asked.

"No, but I wish she were."

Leslie Ann looked up at the banker's wife. "What a nice thing to say."

"Could've fooled me," said the balding little man. "You look like two peas in a pod. Same color hair an' all."

Maddy knew Jasper was being evasive. He already knew Leslie Ann Holmes was a foreign student staying with her and Beau this year. She'd told him about the girl at Ralph Grundy's funeral. That had been months ago, right after Leslie Ann arrived from England. "If you don't want to answer the question, just say so," she said sharply. "We were going to pay you $20 for your time, but if you're not interested –"

"$20 you say –?"

"That's not enough," interjected his wife. As assistant to the mayor, she thought in bigger numbers than the price of a bottle of Wild Boar.

"$40 then," said Maddy. She pulled the money from her purse to show she was willing to pay him on the spot.

"What do you want t' know?" asked Jasper Beanie. She now had his undivided attention, his eyes fixed on the two bills.

"Just what I asked: Did Harley tell you why he killed Sam Buttersworth?"

"Sure he did."

"And –?"

"Said his mother told him to."

159

"His mother —?"

"Yeah, that struck me as funny too. Everybody knows his mother and father been dead for years. Struck by lightning over in the town square. What was that — thirty-some years ago? How could she have told him to do it? I thought he might be crazy, hearing voices of the dead."

"I had a cousin who heard voices," declared Nancy Ann, like it was the most natural thing in the world. "Mostly it was St. Patrick, telling her to watch out for snakes. And she wasn't even Irish."

"Back to Harley," said Maddy. "Did he say why his mother wanted him to kill Sam?"

"No. That's when he offered me $10 to find a box hidden under the bandstand in the town square and deliver it to Mrs. Buttersworth. I got scared and left it on her front steps. I admitted to doing it when the police chief pulled me in that second time — but Harley wouldn't own up to it. Keeping his mouth shut like his lawyer told him to do."

~ ~ ~

"Crazy talk," said Bootsie as they drove back. "Harley claiming he was told to kill Sam by his dead mother. That's like David Burkowitz claiming his neighbor's dog put him up to shooting all those people."

"Or Joan of Arc," added Lizzie. "She heard voices too."

"That was different," said Cookie.

"Jasper's probably suffering from DTs," commented Bootsie. "His brain's been pickled in Wild Boar."

"Do you think Harley's going for an insanity defense?" asked Cookie. She was wedged into the backseat of Bootsie's Toyota with Lizzie and Leslie Ann. Hardly enough room to breathe in this compact little SUV.

"No, Mark the Shark is going to claim suicide," Maddy assured them, comfortable in the passenger seat. "His legal secretary told Tilly that's the plan."

"Be careful of what Doris Grossman says," warned Lizzie. "The old biddy is getting senile. At least that's what Margie Yost says."

"Speaking of Margie," said Maddy, "what exactly did she tell you about Gloria Bradshaw?"

Lizzie tilted her head back with amusement. "Just that Gloria's a big phony, that she never went to Ball State University like she claims."

"Then where *did* she go?" asked Bootsie, eyes on the road. "She certainly left town for a year or so."

"Margie thinks she went to Chi-Town with her brother and his wife."

"What for?"

"To help with the baby," said Lizzie. "That's when Harley was born."

"Why do we care whether Gloria went to college or not?" grumbled Cookie. "What does that have to do with ol' Sam's death?"

"Probably nothing," Lizzie admitted.

"Drop me off at home," sighed Cookie, giving up. "I haven't seen my husband in two days. He will have starved to death by now without me to cook for him."

Maddy looked out the car window at the snowy landscape. It looked bleak, like a moon of Pluto. "You can drop me and Leslie Ann off at the house. Too late to go to church." She and Beau attended Peaceful Meadows, the picturesque church on the far side of the town square. Rev. Copeland was known for his lengthy sermons, a good naptime for many in the congregation.

"If I go to Hell for missing church today, I'll never forgive Jasper Beanie," said Cookie. The most devout of the group, she was a regular at St. Paul's.

"Talking to Jasper Beanie was a waste of time," Bootsie sighed, unable to hide her disappointment. She was more upset at missing brunch at Cozy Café. On Sunday it was buffet-style, eat all you want for $12.95 a person. And that included the dessert table.

"So where does this dead mother come in?" asked Lizzie, checking her lipstick in the car mirror. The shade perfectly matched her lighter red hair. She would have preferred to sleep in, but her friends had insisted she accompany them on what turned out to be a fool's errand.

"Dead mother – that's crazy talk," repeated Bootsie.

"Sounds like Harley's the one who's crazy, talking to his dead mother," opined Maddy. She didn't believe in ghosts and angels and spirits from the "other side."

"What if Harley's mother isn't dead?" Leslie Ann spoke up from the backseat.

"Oh, she's dead for sure," answered Cookie. "Carrie Bradshaw and her husband Emmett were struck by lightning on October 12, 1970. Nothing left of them but ashes and a few stray bones, according to news reports in the *Burpyville Gazette*." Her eidetic memory again.

"But what if Carrie Bradshaw is not Harley's mother?" said the girl. "What if Gloria is?"

Chapter Thirty
Mathematics Quiz

$\mathcal{M}$ADDY MADISON'S Ford Explorer crunched through the snow leading up to the Bradshaw farmhouse. The tires would occasionally spin, seeking traction, but kept moving forward. The outside temperature was far too cold for the snow to melt, so travel remained difficult. Maddy had encountered few cars on the road.

She had drawn the short straw. They figured Gloria would not welcome a committee comprised of all four members of the Quilters Club. After all, Cookie had found her love letters. Bootsie was the police chief's wife. And she'd never got along with Lizzie when they were on the cheerleading squad in high school. But she *might* allow Maddy to get her foot in the door. They had no history between them.

Gloria Bradshaw answered the knock, a frilly apron tied around her waist. She'd been making biscuits and flour stuck to the apron like a light layer of snow. "Maddy Madison, what in the world are you doing out in this weather?" she greeted her visitor.

"Sorry to bother you, Gloria, but I wanted to ask you a few questions without a lot of people around."

"About what? If it has to do with Sam Butterworth, I have nothing more to say. Your friend Cookie Brown found my private letters. So the cat's out of the bag."

"Not quite," said Maddy as she stepped into the warmth

of the living room. A fire crackled in the stone fireplace. Now inside the house, she had gotten farther than Chief Purdue.

"Ask away. But I won't promise to answer them. Don't mind me if I finish rolling my biscuits." She moved into the kitchen, Maddy following a few steps behind. The counter was as white as the farmhouse's yard, a flour-encrusted rolling pin lying next to a large wad of dough.

"You must be planning on baking a lot of biscuits," observed Maddy, noting the size of the unrolled dough ball.

"For the church social. Tomorrow night, if it doesn't snow again."

"The weather girl on Channel 4 said the snow was over for the moment," Maddy replied. "Darlene Baxter is right most of the time."

"She ought to be. I hear she has a degree in meteorology."

"Yes, she attended University of Indiana same year as my daughter Tilly."

"Do tell? I've been a fan of her's ever since she joined the news team two or three years ago."

"Where did *you* go to school?" Maddy slipped in the question as smoothly as a knife cutting melted butter.

Gloria Bradshaw hesitated before answering. "Uh, Ball State. Down in Muncie."

"Good school. What did you major in?"

"Mathematics."

"If X equals 12, what does 2X equal?"

"Huh? I don't know. 6?"

"You didn't go to Ball State, did you? You certainly didn't major in math."

Gloria looked panicky. "What on earth are you talking about, Maddy Madison? You can't come in here and call me a liar straight to my face."

"I remember when you went off to school. Your brother and his wife moved to Chicago about the same time."

"That's right."

"All three of you came back to Caruthers Corners a year later. At least that's what I heard. I was off at school myself."

"I came home 'cause I flunked out of Ball State. That's why I'm not good at math. My studies were caught short." She looked as if about to cry. A wide Band-Aid covered a cut on her forehead from the wreck. He left eye was now purple.

"Emmett and Carrie Bradshaw came back from Chicago with a new baby, as I recall."

"Yes, Harley was born while they were up there in the Windy City. I went up to visit Carrie in the hospital. That's when I decided to drop out of school."

"Drop out? I thought you said you flunked."

"What does it matter?"

"Because I think Harley is your son, not Carrie's. I checked the dates on your love letters. You were in your senior year in high school at the time; Sam Buttersorth was ten years older. I think Sam knocked you up, but couldn't marry you because he was already married to Emmy. So you went off and had the baby and let your brother and his wife claim the child. Then when they got killed in that freak electrical storm, you raised Harley pretending to be his aunt. That must've been very hard for you."

"Damn you, Maddy. Why can't you Quilters Clubbers leave this be?" Her eyes swelled with tears.

"We don't mean to cause you pain, Gloria. But this

explains why Harley ran over ol' Sam. A mercy killing. Sam was eaten up by cancer, but couldn't collect on his new insurance policy if he died from a preexisting condition. So he prevailed on his son to help him out. That way he could leave something to both you and his wife."

"You think you're so smart, don't you?"

"Chief Purdue was puzzled why Sam would include you in his will. Even after he saw the love letters, half a million dollars seemed like a pretty generous sum for an old girlfriend. But maybe it's a reasonable bequest for the mother of his only child."

"If you prove collusion in Sam's death, there won't be any money for anybody. That's why Sam set it up this way."

"Insurance fraud – that's illegal."

"Who are you? I don't see any badge."

"You're willing to sacrifice your son for this cockamamie scheme? He'll do thirty years in prison for murder."

Gloria said, "That's Harley's choice. He was merely honoring his dad's dying wish – not to let him suffer an agonizing death from the ravages of the Big C."

"You're admitting Harley was assisting in a terminal patient's assisted suicide?"

"As Doctor Kevorkian once said, 'Dying is not a crime.' This wasn't murder. It's a case of voluntary euthanasia."

"It's still illegal."

"Not in California, Oregon, Washington, and Vermont."

"But this happened in Caruthers Corners, Indiana. "

"I suggest you read Raymond Whiting's *A Natural Right to Die: Twenty-Three Centuries of Debate*. It argues for legalization."

"May be a little late for that."

Chapter Thirty-One

An Unexpected Invitation

DAN SOKOLOWSKI was pleased with himself. After much effort, he'd succeeded in fixing the grandfather clock. Now it ticked with a steady beat, like the sound of a human heart.

He'd talked with his son this morning, assuring himself that Isaac was having a happy Hanukkah. The diamond trade was going well for him. His wife was healthy, over her bout with the flu. Little Joseph was delighted with the dreidel his grandfather had sent him, an antique top he'd picked up at a flea market. Its sides were marked with the traditional symbols *nun*, *gimel*, *he*, and *shin* – the acronym for "a great miracle happened there."

Joseph was truly a miracle, the grandchild he never expected he'd live to see. He'd been a boy himself when he came as a refugee to America, leaving his home in Dresden. His mother had died in the bombing; his father had died in a camp. He never envisioned the future he now shared with the good people of Caruthers Corners. Life was kind to him.

Ding! Ding!

Sokolowski looked up from his handiwork when the bell over the door tinkled, announcing a potential customer. He was surprised to see that girl, Leslie Ann Holmes.

"My dear, what can I do for you today? Sell you a fine ring? Help you select a belated Christmas gift for a young man?"

"There is no young man," she replied meekly.

"Surely you will be going to the Father Time Dance tomorrow night?"

"No, no one asked me."

"Don't worry, I'm sure someone will. A pretty young lady like you."

"Thank you. If it were only true."

"True is what happens," said the old man.

Leslie Ann forced a smile. "Actually, I came to see you. I brought this plate of watermelon and chocolate cookies. I baked them myself. Mrs. Madison taught me how."

"For me?" Daniel Elisha Sokolowski was taken aback by this gesture of kindness.

"I know you live alone and have no one to bake cookies for you. And it's Hanukkah, I am told."

"Bless you, my child. And I have a gift for you." He reached into a box on the counter and produced a perfect string of pearls. "These will look lovely on you."

"I-I-I cannot accept such an expensive present," she stammered.

"Of course you can. They will be perfect for the Father Time Dance."

The girl looked bewildered. "But I'm not –"

"Yes, you are. You will see."

~ ~ ~

As Leslie Ann Holmes stumbled out of the antiques shop, she nearly collided with someone on the sidewalk. She'd been looking down at the pearl necklace, not watching her step."

"Oh, sorry –" she said quickly.

"Leslie Ann, I've been looking for you."

She glanced up to confront Billy Hofstadter. The boy who lived in the house you could see from space. "Y-you've been looking for me?"

He looked a little embarrassed. "Do you have a date for the dance?"

"N-no."

"Then would you wanna go with me?" He offered a nervous smile.

"Why at this late date? The dance is tomorrow night."

Billy squirmed, hunching up his shoulders. "I've been wanting to ask you. But I just didn't have the courage. You a fine lady from English society; and me the son of a manager at the Family Dollar Store."

"Society?" laughed Leslie Ann. "My father's a collier."

"A what?"

"A coal miner in South Wales. I live in London with my Mum. She works in a millinery shop. My dad comes home every fortnight. We're poor as church mice."

"I'm not entirely sure what you just said, but do you want to go to the dance?"

"Oh yes, I do."

Billy said, "I should warn you, I don't actually know how to dance."

"Don't worry,' she giggled. "I will teach you. It's as easy as shuffling your two left feet."

Chapter Thirty-Two

Contesting the Will

JUST BEFORE TEN Mark And Tilly dropped little Agnes off at the big Victorian on Melon Pickers Lane. They were going shopping in Indy, a day trip. Leslie Ann had volunteered to watch the baby. Carson's was having a pre-January White Sale – 70% off.

"Here are some goodies for the road," said Maddy, handing her daughter a Saran-covered platter of cookies. Watermelon and chocolate, one of her favorites.

"Thanks, Mom. I'll have to fight Mark for these."

"Hey, can I have one now?" he eyed the platter.

"Wait till we get on the road," his wife pulled them away.

"Drive carefully," said Maddy. Always a worrywart. "It's still snowing."

"The worst is over," Mark reassured her. "At least that's what Channel 4 says."

"Doesn't look like it to me." Maddy glanced out the window to emphasize her concern. "Besides, there's still twelve inches of snow on the ground. The roads have to be a mess."

"I've got my snow tires on. And I promise to take it easy."

Tilly said, "Don't worry, Mom. Mark is very good at driving in the snow."

"Well, okay."

Mark handed his daughter over to Leslie Ann. "Take care of Aggie. We'll try to be back by dark."

"I'm surprised you're taking a day off," said Beau. He hadn't left for work yet because he'd promised to help Maddy take down the tree. "Thought you'd be tied up preparing the big defense for Harley Bradshaw."

"It's not such a big defense. Quite simple really. No reason not to tell you, now that Gloria has spilled the beans. Suicide by proxy – a kindness to a father dying of irreversible Stage IV cancer. And I have a Super 8 film that shows Sam Buttersworth deliberately stepping into the path of the vehicle. Free will. He chose to die."

"Do you think it will work?"

"No, not really. But we're going for the sympathy of the jury. It's the only shot for a reduced sentence. I'm thinking ten years, five off for good behavior."

Beau rubbed his chin, as pointed and pitted as Maddy's was round and smooth. "Well, at least there's no motive of malice, now that those family feud stories have been disproven."

Mark paused at the door, a shadow clouding his countenance. He had a square jaw, kind of a Clark Kent face. No wonder Tilly called him "My hero." He said, "That family feud situation may have changed."

"Changed? How so?" asked Maddy.

"Emmy Buttersworth filed to contest the will yesterday. She hired a high-powered lawyer from Indianapolis, a slickster named Barnabas Soltairé. They're claiming Sam wasn't of sound mind when he had me draw up the will a few weeks ago. He'll be using my suicide defense as proof of Sam's poor judgment, his addled state of mind."

"Sounds like a Catch-22. If Sam was crazy, the will's broken and Gloria doesn't get the money. If he's not crazy, then he consciously colluded in his own murder and Gloria doesn't get the money."

"That's about it."

"Gloria Bradshaw won't be happy getting cut out of the will," observed Maddy. She recalled her recent visit, the manic nature of Harley's aunt – well, his mother as it turns out.

"No, she's not. I've already had about ten phone calls from her. That's one reason I'm taking today off. Getting outta Dodge, as they say."

~ ~ ~

Maddy had picked that morning to take down the Christmas decorations. She wasn't one of those types who left the wreath on the front door until July. When it was over, it was over. Move on to the next holiday. New Year's Father Time Dance coming up.

She removed the ornaments from the Christmas tree, handing them to Leslie Ann, who carefully placed them into their compartmentalized boxes. Then together they unstrung the colored lights, storing them in a plastic box till next year.

Beau dismantled the tree. It looked almost real. This was the first year they'd not had a genuine Douglas fir. Beau missed the smell, that acrid piney scent that he identified with Christmas.

"How's the baby?" Maddy asked as she pulled down the garland surrounding the doorways. Little Agnes was in her playpen in the next room. Her Grammy kept one there for her visits.

"Still sleeping," reported Leslie Ann. "A little angel."

Beau chuckled. "Not if she wakes up. That little tot's got a set of lungs on her. Maybe she'll grow up to be an opera singer."

"In that case I'll start her rehearsing Mozart's '*O zittre nicht, mein lieber Sohn*' later today,'" teased Maddy.

"She can certainly hit the high notes," Leslie Ann smiled.

Maddy removed the little ceramic village that lined the mantle, wrapping each house in tissues and packing it away in a carton. The tiny people – carolers, strollers, skaters, a snowman – got a separate box, their own cardboard dormitory.

When she started removing the Christmas cards taped along the edge of the mantle, Leslie Ann offered, "Here, let me help you with that." But the girl's eager hands brushed the tall green nutcracker perched on a corner of the mantle and it toppled over, falling down-down-down onto the hearth. *Krak!* – it bounced off the uneven stones.

The wooden soldier's mouth flew open, as if silently yelping in pain. A tip of his curved moustache broke off, skittering across the oak floor. A round wooden plug popped out of the bottom of his feet, as if losing the heel of a shoe.

"Ooo, I'm sorry," squealed the girl. "I broke Beau's nutcracker."

"Don't worry," he said, scooping it up. "Only thing broken is the tip of the moustache. I can glue that back on, you'd never know it happened."

As Beau held the wooden soldier up by his hat, a piece of paper slithered out of the hole in the bottom. The plug had hidden a chamber inside the wooden Christmas

174

ornament. "What have we here?" he muttered, picking up the paper.

"A secret message," joked his wife. "Maybe it's Santa's list of who's been naughty and who's been nice."

"What does it really say?" asked Leslie Ann.

Beau unfolded the paper and read the words aloud:

"My Dearest Minnie,

"I am sending you this nutcracker as a thank-you for buying my quilt last year. The $20 was most needed at the time. I had been unemployed due to the closing of the hosiery mill. My husband carved this steadfast wooden soldier with his own hands. We are a most talented family as you see, Roger with his carving knife, me with my quilting needles, even my cousin Thomas with his drawings. Thomas is planning to study at the National Academy of Design when he can save up enough for the tuition. He gave me the design for your Christmas quilt. Originally, he provided an image of Brother Jonathan; however when I told him you wanted a Christmas quilt he added a white beard and a pointed stocking cap. I was right pleased how it turned out. I am so happy that you liked it. Indeed I miss our years together at boarding school. Madam Hanover made her best effort to teach us etiquette and manners. I wish more of it had stuck.

Your faithful friend,
Sarah"

"Sarah?" said his wife. "Do you think –?"

"Of course, it's Sarah Soldemeir. The letter mentions my great-grandmother's Christmas quilt."

"And your great-grandmother was named Minerva. Minnie might have been her nickname."

"That letter must have been inside the nutcracker for many, many years," noted Leslie Ann. "It's surprising no one ever found it."

"Who would have suspected this old chunk of wood had a hollow core," shrugged Beau, turning the nutcracker so he could look it in the painted eyes.

"Well, this solves one historical mystery. Sarah's cousin – the young Thomas Nast – did have an influence on the quilt. The design started out to be Uncle Sam, which explains the striped pants and star-spangled coat."

"Wait! The letter doesn't mention Uncle Sam," protested the girl. "It says he gave her a drawing of Brother Jonathan, whomever that might be."

Maddy smiled. The British girl couldn't be expected to know Early American history. But if she stayed here long enough, Cookie would correct that shortcoming. "In the 1850s, the names Brother Jonathan and Uncle Sam were used interchangeably," Maddy explained, factoids she'd learned while Googling about Thomas Nast.

"Was there a real Brother Jonathan?" asked Leslie Ann.

"Likely not. The term came into use during the Revolutionary War, a symbol for long-winded New Englanders. Cartoonists dressed him in striped trousers, a black coat, and stove-pipe hat."

"Just like your Uncle Sam?"

"Some say Uncle Sam was the depiction of a man

named Samuel Wilson, who was a well-know purveyor to troops during the War of 1812. His nickname of Uncle Sam became conflated with goods stamped U.S., meaning United States. Eventually, the fictional Uncle Sam took on the same costume as Brother Jonathan and the two merged into a national personification of the United States."

Now she had Beau's curiosity. "Where did Thomas Nast come in?"

"He drew lots of political cartoons for *Frank Leslie's Illustrated Newspaper* and *Harper's Weekly*. He often used Uncle Sam to symbolize the United States."

"So my great-grandmother and Sarah Soldemeir went to boarding school together," Beau said. "Roommates, I'd guess."

"That's the connection between your family and a semi-famous quiltmaker," his wife nodded. "And by extension with political cartoonist Thomas Nast."

"Another mystery solved," grinned the girl. Taking credit for the end result of her clumsiness. "I guess I might make a detective yet."

"A regular Sherlock Holmes."

"I think I'll stick to being Leslie Ann Holmes."

~ ~ ~

Leslie Ann asked permission to use Maddy's iMac. She was curious about this character called Santa Claus. Was he the same as Father Christmas, the tall, bearded gift-giver she'd known in London.

With a couple of clicks, she had the history:

"Father Christmas is the traditional British name for the personification of the December holiday. Although now associated with the American Santa Claus, he is actually

part of an unrelated and much older English folkloric tradition. Father Christmas himself first appeared in the mid-17th Century in the aftermath of the English Civil War. Puritans had tried to abolish Christmas, but Royalists adopted Old Father Christmas as the symbol of 'the good old days' of feasting and good cheer. However, in Victorian times the holiday became more children-oriented and Father Christmas morphed into a bringer of gifts."

She was glad to learn she had her own Father Christmas, although it had been fun to pretend in Santa Claus along with her American "second family." At fifteen, she understood both were fanciful myths. But in her imagination, she would take the lanky Beauregard Madison as her Father Christmas over that rotund Fatty Johnson, red suit or not.

Part 3

The Last of the Spirits

"The Phantom slowly, gravely, silently approached. When it came, Scrooge bent down upon his knee; for in the very air through which this Spirit moved it seemed to scatter gloom and mystery."

- Charles Dickens, *A Christmas Carol*

Chapter Thirty-Three

Oranges and Lemons

" A GOOD PIECE of detective work, our figuring out that Gloria Bradshaw was Harley's mother," Maddy was saying to Leslie Ann as they sipped their soup. The girl had never had hot watermelon soup before. American meals were always a new experience. No bangers and mash or black pudding. No steak and kidney pie or mushy peas.

"I figured it out," she reminded Maddy. Wanting credit where credit was due.

Maddy smiled tolerantly. "Yes, I meant *you* as a member of the Quilters Club team."

That pleased Leslie Ann. "Does that mean I can be a full-fledged member?"

"Until you go back to London," Maddy nodded. As if the informal quilting bee had membership levels.

"Supercalifragilisticexpialidocious!" the girl squealed.

"As I was saying, in spite of all your brilliant detecting, we missed one thing."

The smile turned to a frown. "Missed something?"

"You'll remember Jasper Beanie had told us Harley said his mother told him to do it. Murder ol' Sam, that is."

The girl nodded slowly. "Yes, that's true."

" ... and that would mean?"

"That Gloria Bradshaw is the one behind the murder. She told Harley to do it!"

"Well, that's Jasper's version. But he's an old sot.

Drinks a lot of that cheap whiskey. Question is, can we accept his word on what Harley told him?"

"But it makes sense, doesn't it. Given all we now know."

"Yes, but we need to make certain before we tell the police."

The redhead slurped up the last few drops of her soup. "Then let's go brace Gloria Bradshaw and see what she has to say."

Maddy nodded. "Maybe that is the thing to do. If I'm not back within an hour, call Chief Purdue and tell him where I am."

"Wait. You cannot go without me. You said I was a full-fledged member."

"Yes, but someone has to watch little Agnes."

You could almost see the wheels turning inside Leslie Ann's pretty little head. "I have it. Let's ask the Andrews sisters to come over and watch Agnes for an hour. Mary and Catherine babysit all the time. They're practically professionals."

~ ~ ~

Simon Andrews and his wife Rebecca owned a modest cottage at the far end of Easy Chair Lane. He was day manager at the nearby E-Z Chair factory, the biggest manufacturing concern in Caruthers Corners. It was known for its Amish-style straight back chairs. There was a big Amish community in this part of Indiana. On your way to Burpyville you had to watch out for all the slow-moving horse-drawn buggies with triangular reflectors on the back. A peaceful community that shunned modern-day conveniences, the Amish largely kept to themselves.

The Andrew twins were Leslie Ann's age, a strange pair

who looked like those eerie girls standing in the hallway of the Overlook Hotel in *The Shining*. The girls' parents encouraged their friendship with the new British student, concerned that they were too insular. Sometimes twins are like that. Making up their own languages and finishing each other's sentences. Leslie Ann's bubbly personality seemed to bring the girls out of their shell.

So when Leslie Ann phoned to ask if they could babysit little Agnes, their parents said, "Yes, of course."

~ ~ ~

Gloria Bradshaw opened the door to Maddy's knock, her eyes as wild as a cornered bobcat. "What do you want now?" she demanded.

"I brought you some watermelon soup," she offered, holding out a covered pot. Food was the passport for gaining entry to any household in Caruthers Corners.

Gloria eyed the offering warily. "Soup?"

"It's piping hot." Last of the batch she'd shared with Leslie Ann at lunch. Beau would have to do without. But he'd agree this was a worthwhile sacrifice.

"The soup is quite delicious," Leslie Ann spoke up, nearly hidden behind Maddy's thick coat. Snow swirled in the yard behind them, the storm trying to reassert itself.

"Come in, I suppose." The door swung inward to allow them entry.

Maddy and her ward shuffled inside. The living room was small, crowded with a Naugahyde couch and La-Z-Boy recliner. A black velvet painting of Elvis hung on the wall along with a copy of the Lord's Prayer.

"Must be 20° out there," commented Maddy.

"Cold as the grave," Gloria nodded solemnly. A strange

expression. Her injured eye gave her a raccoon look. The pupils were dilated. Maddy wondered if the woman might be on something – Ketamine or speed.

Gloria took the pot from Maddy and set it on the kitchen counter. "I suppose you've heard that Emmy Buttersworth's trying to break the will."

"Yes, I have. Perhaps she will change her mind. She's likely angry after learning of your relationship with her husband."

"Emmy should be thankful that I've stayed away from him all these years. It was me who broke it off, not Sam."

"I heard he refused to leave his wife."

"That's hogwash," spat Gloria. "It was me who wouldn't let him leave his wife. I'm not a home wrecker."

"No, you clearly aren't," said Maddy. Better to agree, she told herself.

"Emmy's hired some high-powered lawyer named Barnabas Soltairé. I hear he's mob-connected. Don't surprise me she'd stoop so low. The things Sam told me about her. She's not the wounded saint everybody makes her out to be."

"What about Harley. She liked him. Told me so herself. Surely she won't cut him out of his inheritance from his father."

"Haw! Emmy probably doesn't think so highly of the boy now she knows he's Sam's son by me. And there's the fact that Harley killed Sam. No, she's out to stick it to both me and my boy."

Harley was hardly a boy at thirty-three. That was a reminder of how much time had passed since the affair between his mother and Emmy Buttersworth's husband.

But some injuries are difficult to get over, it would seem. "I know my son-in-law will fight hard to protect your rights. He drew up the will and won't let some Indy ambulance chaser overthrow it without a fight. After all, his reputation is on the line."

"Mark Tidemore's going to have his hands full defending Harley's murder charge. You think he'll pay enough attention to that will? He hasn't returned my phone calls all day."

"Oh, didn't you know? He's out of town."

"He can stay there for all I care. I'm going to take matters in my own hands. Emmy better give me my money. It's small compensation for all the years I devoted to raising her husband's son."

Maddy was taken aback at this new tone. "Didn't Sam help out with his son's upbringing? He certainly spent time with Harley, taking him fishing, inviting him into his home."

"Sam slipped me money on the side. My brother's estate wasn't as big as most people thought. We couldn't have made it without Sam's support. But Harley's a grown man now and the money stopped coming over a decade ago. This was a way to pay me back for all the sacrifices I've made. That's the way I explained it to Sam when I asked him to take out the insurance policy. Fact is, it was *all* supposed to come to me, but he got namby-pamby at the last minute and left half to Emmy. Now that greedy old biddy wants it all for herself."

Maddy didn't know what to make of this vituperous speech. Gloria verged on the unhinged. Perhaps it was time to go.

"Leslie Ann and I just dropped by to pay our respects. I hope you like the watermelon soup. It's my own personal recipe."

"You don't fool me, Maddy Madison. You didn't come out here in this blizzard to bring me some soup. You're a spy for Emmy Buttersworth."

"No, that's not –"

"'Tis true," Gloria Bradshaw interrupted. "Well, I have a message for you to carry back to that harridan. Tell her I said, 'Oranges and Lemons.' She'll know what it means."

Now the woman was talking crazy. Even Leslie Ann looked upset by the nonsensical rambling. "No need to see us out," Maddy hustled the girl to the front door. "We have to get home. The snow's picking up."

Chapter Thirty-Four

A Frozen Pilgrimage

A WILLOWY TEEN, Leslie Ann favored Twill button-down blouses and short A-line skirts with thick leggings underneath. A nod to modesty, as well as being practical in this cold weather. London could be chilly, but the winters in Indiana were downright freezing. The average temperature in Indianapolis for December was 26°F, but this year was proving even colder.

On a recent shopping trip to Kohl's in Indy, Maddy had helped the girl select a ZeroXposur Coleen Hooded Puffer, a full-length coat with ThermoCloud insulation. It made her look like the Pillsbury Doughboy, but it was warm.

Leslie Ann glanced out the kitchen window at the thermometer Beau had mounted outside. Barely 10° it said. *Brrrrr* indeed.

"Please may I go over to the Andrews' house after I help with the dishes?" asked Leslie Ann, always formally polite. "I want to thank them for babysitting Agnes." Back from Indianapolis, Mark and Tilly had just picked up their daughter.

"Don't worry about the dishes," said Maddy. "I'll finish them up. Be sure to wear your heavy coat and boots. It's still cold out there."

"Yes ma'am."

The Andrews family lived only two blocks away, if you cut across Field Hand Alley. Otherwise Maddy would have worried about the girl being out in this weather. The radio confirmed the storm wasn't over.

Maddy watched Leslie Ann skitter down the walkway, disappearing into the blustering snow. Beau had shoveled the walk only this morning but it was already covered with an inch or two of snow.

Leslie Ann had promised to call when she got to the Andrews' to report that she'd arrived safely. You couldn't take any chances in weather like this.

~ ~ ~

The girl trudged across the town square, the snow calf-high on her boots. It was coming down like white granules of salt from an overturned shaker. She could barely make out the looming shape of the bandstand as she passed it. She knew Mrs. Madison would be upset with her if she'd known about this secret pilgrimage.

Rather than going to the Andrews' house, she'd deviated her path toward Main Street, only a few blocks farther to the right. The police station was just past the Cozy Café. As she grew near, she could make out the boxy shape of the building. She hoped Chief Purdue would listen to her. She hated it when adults treated her like a silly child.

It wasn't safe to be out in weather like this, she told herself as her head began to spin and she collapsed in the snow.

~ ~ ~

Chief Jim Purdue looked at the nearly frozen girl, standing there in front of his desk, shivering like a wet Chihuahua. "Leslie Ann, what are you doing out in this weather? Does Maddy know you're here?"

"She thinks I'm at the Andrews' house with Mary and

Catherine. I was afraid she wouldn't allow me to come this far in the snow."

"With good reason. If Pete Hitzer hadn't spotted you there at the edge of the town square you'd be an icicle by now."

With the deputy's thick watch coat wrapped around her, color was returning to her cheeks. "But I had to deliver a message to you," she insisted. "It's a matter of life and death."

"Whose life, whose death?"

"Emmy Buttersworth. You must go out to her house right away. She's in grave danger."

Chief Purdue smiled at the girl. "Now, honey, I'm sure Emmy is just fine. Harley's locked up."

"Harley is not the threat. It's his mother."

"What makes you think Gloria Bradshaw wants to harm Emmy?"

"She made a threat against her. I heard it."

"Really? You heard Gloria threaten Sam's wife?"

"Yes, she told Maddy to give Emmy a message. It was a death threat, that she would chop off her head if she didn't get her half of the inheritance."

"She said that?"

"Actually, she said, 'Oranges and Lemons.'"

"Oranges and what? Apples? What's fruit got to do with this?"

"'Oranges and Lemons,'" she corrected. "It's a British nursery rhyme."

"So how's that a threat?"

"Nursery rhymes are often not about what they sound like. Frequently they have a hidden meaning."

He frowned. "'Humpty Dumpty' isn't about an egg falling off a wall?"

"Actually it's about a big cannon."

"'Mary Mary, Quite Contrary'?"

"It's about Bloody Mary, daughter of Henry VIII. She behaved 'quite contrary' to England's wishes, trying to force the country to become Catholic again."

"'Ring Around the Rosie'?"

"About the bubonic plague. 'We all fall down.'"

"Holy bejeebers. They teach children this stuff in London?"

"Mother Goose may have been a wicked witch," she exaggerated.

"So what makes this 'Oranges and Lemons' remark a threat?"

"It's a rhyme about someone trying to collect money owed them. The last verse contains a death threat."

"And you're saying Gloria is sending Emmy a warning about trying to cut her out of the will?"

"Exactly. Her life is in danger. Miss Bradshaw may have had more to do with Sam Buttersworth's death than you think."

"You mean she put Harley up to killing ol' Sam?"

"She admitted it to us," the girl nodded.

"About this 'Oranges and Lemons' poem, I don't know it."

"Let me recite it. I think you will see the intended message." Leslie Ann cleared her throat, then delivered the nursery rhyme in a child-like sing-song voice:

"Oranges and lemons
Say the bells of St Clemens,
You owe me five farthings,
Say the bells of St Martin,
When will you pay me?
Say the bells of Old Bailey,
When I grow rich,
Say the bells of Shoreditch,
When will that be?
Say the bells of Stepney,
I do not know
Says the great bell of Bow.

Here comes a candle to light you to bed
And here comes a chopper
To chop off your head!
Chip, chop, chip, chop
The last one is dead!"

"I get it," nodded the police chief. "Gloria is saying if Emmy doesn't share the inheritance, □ she will murder her, just like she did with Sam."

"That about sums it up," said Leslie Ann Holmes in her best British accent.

Chapter Thirty-Five

And Here Comes A Chopper

POLICE CHIEF Jim Purdue agreed to drive out to Emmy Buttersworth's farmhouse and make sure she was okay. A "wellness call," in police parlance. Better play it safe, even if he thought the girl's fantastical tale about nursery rhymes was a bunch of hooey. "Ring Around the Rosie" being about the bubonic plague – ha!

He volunteered to drop the girl off at the Madison house on his way. Melon Pickers Lane wasn't more than two blocks out of the way as he headed out to Highway 21. Maddy would be worrying about her young guest, having discovered she wasn't at the Andrews house from his phone call.

Leslie Ann hunkered down in the backseat, wrapped in her Hooded Puffer. She was a tad nervous, not so much that Maddy Madison would be angry with her, but more due to the fact she's never been in the back of a police car before. There was a grill between her and Chief Purdue. And there were no handles on the inside of the doors. She felt like a criminal ... or maybe she was feeling guilty over telling Maddy she was going to visit the Andrews twins.

When the cruiser pulled into the Madisons' wide driveway, the front door opened and Maddy hurried through the snow toward them. "I'm going with you," she announced as she slid into the front seat.

"You'd best get Leslie Ann inside and thaw her out. I'm

sure there's nothing to worry about at the Buttersworth farm. The girl just got carried away with her imagination, I'd say."

"Perhaps, but no point in taking a chance. Gloria Bradshaw looked pretty weird when she told me to deliver that 'Oranges and Lemons' message to Emmy."

"Did you?"

"Did I what?"

"Deliver the message."

"No, I haven't seen Emmy since we were out there about the dueling pistols. That's why I'm going with you now, to deliver the message."

"Seems kind of silly, giving her the name of a nursery rhyme."

"But that's the message Gloria asked me to deliver. I didn't give it much thought till you phoned me a few minutes ago and told me about Leslie Ann being at the police station."

"I knew it was a threat the minute she said 'Oranges and Lemons,'" whimpered the girl from the backseat.

"Oh," said Maddy, almost as if she'd forgotten that Leslie Ann was in the cruiser. "Then why didn't you tell me, dear? I would have driven you to the police station myself. Jim said his deputy found you in a heap in the snow. You could have died of hypothermia!"

"I'm sorry, I should have. But I was afraid you'd think I was being daffy."

Chief Purdue eyed her in the backseat. "And you didn't think I'd consider it daffy?"

"Maybe, but we're driving out to Emmy Buttersworth's farmhouse, aren't we?"

"Well, yes —" Jim Purdue squinched up his face as if silently reprimanding himself. Outflanked by a child.

~ ~ ~

The scene was blinding white, snow filling the air, but Maddy could make out the vague shape of an automobile. "Is that Emmy's car?" she asked.

"No, Emmy drives a Ford Fairlane," said the police chief. "There's no garage. Sam always parked it in the barn during bad weather."

"Then whose car —?"

"Looks like Leslie Ann was right," Jim Purdue admitted. "That's Gloria Bradshaw's Chevy Impala. You can make out the scrapes along the bottom from where she ran it into a field the other day. Went off the road on the Highway 21 Bypass. Evers Gochnauer said she was doing nearly 80 in the middle of the blizzard."

"Are we too late?" asked Leslie Ann from the backseat.

"Don't know, honey. You gals stay here. I'll see what's going on." He opened the car door, ducking his head against the snow, unholstering his service revolver, a .38 Smith & Wesson. This was the first time he'd ever drawn the gun in his entire career as a policeman.

"I'm coming with you," said Maddy, reaching for her door handle.

"No, you stay put. We don't know what I'm gonna find in there." His boots sank deeply into the snow as he climbed the path toward the farmhouse. He could make out the faint impression of footprints ahead of him.

The front door was cracked open. That was odd, given the sub-zero temperature out here. He used a mittened finger to push it open, keeping his pistol tightly gripped in his right hand.

"Emmy, are you home?" he shouted into the house.

No answer.

He stepped into the foyer. "Gloria, are you here?"

"Stay away," came a voice.

Police chief Jim Purdue turned the corner into the living room. There was Gloria Bradshaw standing over Sam's wife, arm raised, ready to plunge a butcher knife into her throat.

The words of the nursery rhyme rang in his head:

"And here comes a chopper
To chop off your head!"

Gloria's arm came down with the speed of a striking snake.

Chief Purdue pulled the trigger.

Chapter Thirty-Six

The Jury's Verdict

JIM PURDUE was not a very good shot. He missed Gloria Bradshaw by a good two yards, ricocheting off a metal vase and shattering a window. But the sound of the gunshot frightened the deranged blonde so badly she dropped to the floor in a dead faint.

Disaster averted. Emmy Buttersworth hadn't been injured, but she was very frightened. She couldn't stop shaking.

The police chief called his dispatcher on the cruiser's radio, requesting that Pete Hitzer come out to the Buttersworth farm to pick up a prisoner.

~ ~ ~

Nearly a year later a jury down in Indy found Gloria Bradshaw and her son Harley guilty of premeditated murder. They were tried together. She got 20 years; Harley got 30. After all, he'd been driving the tractor.

The prosecutor made the case that Gloria had talked Sam Buttersworth into taking out a $1,000,000 life insurance policy with the intent of having her son murder him.

The crazy thing is that Sam, dying of cancer, went along with the plan. He thought it was an act of mercy, his beloved son helping him avoid an agonizing death from the ravages of cancer. The idea of Harley running over him during the Christmas Parade was a way of assuring the insurance would pay off the claim. No death from a preexisting condition. No obvious act of suicide.

At trial, Gloria told a different story. She still hated Sam for dumping her when she got pregnant thirty-four years ago. Harley resented him for never publically acknowledging him as his biological son. And – oh yes – there was all that money to be had.

Psychological testing showed Harley had a diminished capacity to know right from wrong. Mental disorder is an "excuse" for one's wrongful actions. The M'Naghten Rule provides that a person must be suffering from "a defect of reason, from disease of the mind, as not to know the nature and quality of the act he was doing...." Exemption from full criminal punishment on such grounds dates back to the Hammurabi Code. Harley was sent to Central State Hospital instead of prison. He viewed this as that vacation he'd imagined. No palm trees, but the food was good.

His condition was blamed on a high school football injury. But most folks attributed it to living all those years with Gloria.

Gloria showed no repentance. She kept saying Sam Buttersworth agreed to die in order to provide her with the money she deserved for raising his son. She claimed Sam planned it all, but nobody – especially the jury – believed her.

Given the outcome of the trial, Emmy Buttersworth's attorney had no trouble breaking the will. It seemed clear to the judge that Sam Buttersworth had not be in his right mind when he signed the will, knowing that he was playing a part in his own eminent death.

Not having to split the farm with Gloria, Emmy sold off the back forty to Bob Brown for enough money to assure her future. Bob planned to plant watermelons.

Mark Tidemore took the loss gracefully. No way he could have won this one in the State of Indiana. Bartholomew Dingley patted his protégé on the back and said, "You can't win them all." Good advice for a young lawyer.

𝕰pilogue

A Family Reunion

BUT THAT CAME MUCH LATER.
Immediately after Police Chief Jim Purdue arrested Gloria, the world seemed to right itself. The snow stopped, putting an official end to the Great Snowstorm of '02. The stores along Main Street reopened for business: Family Dollar was having a half-price sale on Christmas merchandise. The Dairy Queen was having a special on blizzards. Cozy Café announced a new menu for the New Year; it looked exactly like the old menu, other than it had raised its prices. Ace Hardware was experiencing a high return rate for unwanted Christmas presents (mostly fondue pots which had failed to make a comeback).

The Father Time Dance was getting lots of promotion on the radio from Howlin' Horace.

Roads were clear.

~ ~ ~

It was on New Year's Eve that a taxi pulled up in front of the big three story Victorian on Melon Pickers Lane, disgorging a singular passenger. Beau Madison answered the knock at the door in his stocking feet. He'd closed the hardware store early to get ready for the New Year's Father Time Dance at the high school.

"Hello, brother," the stranger at the door greeted him.

"Mikey," said Beau, shocked to see an older version of his brother Mycroft standing on his front step.

"May I come in?" A suitcase, one of those old-fashioned types, covered in travel stickers, rested beside him. The Great Snowstorm of '02 had passed days ago, and behind him the street was a winter wonderland.

"Of course, of course." Beau turned to yell over his shoulder, "Maddy, cancel all plans. We have company."

Maddy came around the corner from the dining room, a puzzled look on her round face. "Who –?"

"It's my brother Mikey. Call Tilly. Tell her and Mark to get over here. Call everybody – Jim and Bootsie, Cookie and Bob, Lizzie and Edgar – and tell them to forget the dance. There's going to be a party here at the Madison house tonight."

Mycroft Madison held up his hands in gentle protest. "No, no, don't change your plans on account of me. I dropped by without warning. It was an impulse. I thought before I start my new life in Florida, I should set in order my old life in Indiana."

"Come on in," Beau ushered his brother inside. He picked up the heavy suitcase and brought it along to the living room. "I'm so happy to see you, Mikey."

"You got the Christmas quilt and the green nutcracker?"

"Yes indeed. And my wife Maddy and her Quilters Club pals have traced down its history. It's quite a story."

"Do tell. I've always wondered about it. The only clue being that invoice from some woman named Soldedarie or Solmeyer or Sol –"

"Sarah Soldemeir," Maddy supplied. "She was a famous quilter. Related to the political cartoonist Thomas Nast. The quilt claims some small historical significance in its early depiction of Santa Claus."

"I always wondered about that. He looked like St. Nick wearing Uncle Sam's duds."

"That's the interesting part. We'll tell you all about it over dinner."

"How long can you stay?" Maddy asked. "You boys have so much to catch up on."

"Not very long. I have places to go and promises to keep. Besides, Mom always said, 'After three days both fish and guests start to smell.'"

"I remember that," Beau smiled. "But we've had a very cold winter. I think fish – as well as you – will last a little longer than that."

"We'll see."

Just then Leslie Ann Holmes came tiptoeing down the carpeted stairway, so quiet they almost didn't notice her. A teenage boy followed her. Mycroft looked up: "My goodness, is this my niece?"

"No," said the girl politely. "But we can pretend so, if you like."

"Leslie Ann is visiting us from London," Maddy explained. "But she's become one of the family."

"Your niece Matilda – Tilly, we call her – will be over shortly with her new baby Agnes and her husband Mark the Shark," added Beau.

"And this young man?"

Leslie Ann blushed. "This is ... my boyfriend, Billy."

"Hello, hello," said Mycroft. "I can't wait to meet everyone."

"This is going to be a great family reunion," gushed Beau, tears welling in his pale blue eyes.

Maddy smiled at her old Pooh Bear, thinking she'd never seen him so happy.

Leslie Ann smiled and asked in her best British accent, "Is this where I'm supposed to say, 'God bless us, every one' —?"

Thank you for reading. Please review this book. Reviews help others find Absolutely Amazing eBooks and inspire us to keep providing these marvelous tales. If you would like to be put on our email list to receive updates on new releases, contests, and promotions, please go to AbsolutelyAmazingEbooks.com and sign up.

Bonus

By going to the Absolutely Amazing eBooks online website (AbsolutelyAmazingEbooks.com) and entering the password below into the Bonus Reward Section, you can access recipes for many of the dishes you read about in this book – for free!

AA1055

About the Author

Marjory Sorrell Rockwell says needlecraft arts — quilting, crocheting, knitting — are pastimes every woman can appreciate. And she particularly loves quiltmaking. "It's like painting with cloth," she says. But when not quilting she writes mysteries about a Midwestern sleuth not unlike herself, a middle-aged lady with an unpredictable family and loyal friends. And she's a big fan of watermelon pie.

www.ingramcontent.com/pod-product-compliance
Lightning Source LLC
Chambersburg PA
CBHW071040050125
19939CB00043B/1312